My Name is Rose:

Diary of a Serial Killer

THE MADNESS OF ROSE
Dark Diaries Book 1

By Shannon Anton

Stellium Books
Grant Park, Illinois 60940

i

Cover Art by Jaime Rayon
Cover Design by Annette Munnich

www.stelliumbooks.com
Copyright 2015 © Shannon Anton
All rights reserved
Manufactured in the United States
ISBN: 978-0692547809

DEDICATION

I dedicate this to everyone who has
stood by me and watched as this
book grew from a thought, to one
notebook, to many notebooks, and
nights with Icy Hot sitting up with my
cat while trying to complete
chapters.

Dear Jenny
Teagan;
Thank you so much
for the Love &
Support
Shannon

My Name is Rose: Diary of a Serial Killer is a work of fiction. Any resemblance to any actual people is coincidental and unintentional.

TABLE OF CONTENTS

#

There are no clocks in here. No calendar. No date. No anything to tell me how long I've been kept... I got up from my cot and looked in the mirror today. It was a cracked sliver. I could see my eyes; that's about it. There's a sink in here and a toilet. God, I've been locked up in here for so long...

Today the guard asked me if I finally wanted to confess my crimes. They handed me paper and a pen to write them down. I started writing this instead. The only crime I can come up with for myself is the fact that I smell. The guard said no soap in my cell, because I might ingest it. But they let me have a pen? What if I stabbed myself?

I still ask everyday why they brought me here. The guard laughed and said "I should know... but I don't." This is so confusing. We have male guards for a women's area. They're rude too. They poke and prod women. I hear whispers through the walls. I hear the screams and zapping sounds and the sobs of people falling asleep after they've been tortured. An insane thing to fall asleep to, I know, but, what are you going to do when you're trapped? Nothing.

Back to the thing about my crimes. I remember being in a house. I had a family. I had a life. I did P.T.A. and was a soccer mom, until they took me. Were my crimes being there for my children? Shit! If that's a crime you can burn all of us at the stake! That couldn't be why they put me here, is it? Are all the people in here mothers?

Did they rip us out of our homes and leave our children motherless?

My kids. Oh, their faces are burned in my mind. I missed them. I cried for them for weeks when they first brought me here. My son was 13 when they took me. He is tall. I am 5'6 and at 13, he was already an inch taller, grey eyed and quick. He was the star on his soccer team. My daughter was... is... I can only imagine that she still is... at the top of her class.

How long was I in here for again? The guard won't tell me the date. He won't even tell me how many days I've been here. He just repeats himself and says that I need to repent and admit my crimes.

I think that I've done enough writing for today. I'm going to rest my hand. Maybe the guard will give me more paper tomorrow so I can tell you more of this story. Maybe it will help jog my memory as well. Who knows what could happen?

#

I woke up and stretched this morning; that was the longest night's sleep I've had in a while. Maybe it's because I talked to paper and wrote this out for whoever is going to read it in the future. They probably won't. They will more than likely throw this out along with me. I looked down at my shirt and read it. It's a cotton dark green and a v neck. That's what I have to wear in here. They took my clothes when I arrived. The numbers on my shirt read A 0625. I guess that's what they refer to me in here as. My name at one point was really pretty; it was Rose. They don't know. All they know is that I'm guilty of something. I'd like to know what my crimes were. Yesterday I was telling you; yes I know that this is just a piece of paper I'm writing on but someone could read it later and know what hell they put us through in here.

I digress. Tonight I'm going to tell you a little about the night that they took me and brought me here. I was with my husband and we had a date night. There was some movie he had wanted to see. God what was the title? It will come to me sooner or later. This was a nice little walk down memory lane. My husband was 5'9 to my 5'6, with lighter hair than my own, and amazing blue eyes that I could get lost in for hours. In fact I had gotten lost in them many times. Maybe that was why we had two wonderful kids. That was just my stab at humor seeing if there was anything left after being locked up for so long.

Later that night we were in bed. We had turned the lights out and were lying down. That's when they came. All clad in black with guns. They said my name and I screamed. They told my husband that I was evil and to forget all about me.

When he read me my rights, he told me afterwards that for everything I'd done, I should have no rights. There was a laundry list of crimes that I was in trouble for. I was wanted in 35 of 50 states and 17 countries. For what though? They didn't say or did they and I'm blanking out? There are a lot of blanks.

When they brought me here they hooked me up to a chair. There were all these wires and tapes that connected the wires to me. The shocks are like no other pain that I can describe. I can see myself jolting in my chair. Shock therapy it's called I think? There's still some faint scarring on my upper chest from it. It felt like I couldn't drink enough water for days after that to feel right. I don't wish that treatment on anyone. The questions they asked.. Who are you? Where were you born? Things like that over and over. They said I was lying. I am not a liar. I never once lied to my kids, ever!

That's enough for tonight. I'm sure you are tired of hearing about this. Tomorrow I'll talk to you more about my kids and how amazing they are. You don't want to hear about how they think I'm a total psychopath. I think that's what they are. To be completely honest with you, no one just raids a home during the middle of the night and takes you away to a maximum security facility. No one. Until tomorrow...

Day Three

Today was a really long day. The guard read through everything that I've been writing to you the last few days. They took me back to interrogation. They thought it was a confession of guilt. The only thing I'm trying to remember is my life. The shocks don't help much, they sort of hinder the process but I don't think they are smart enough to understand that... Being locked in a room with no one to talk to day in and day out, you are silent because if you scream they come and check on you and then they give you something to really scream about. And then you scream until you can't scream anymore..

I've heard whispers in the halls of someone being injected with something so she couldn't talk anymore. Yeah, no thanks. I'm good. I'll keep silent and just write. Even if they think it's a confession it gives me something to do other than just sit here and stare at the walls at night and try to sleep. You would think that it would be easy to sleep when you haven't done anything all day but it's really not because you have nothing to reflect upon, nothing productive that you've done to think about what so ever. It's kind of lame but it's the truth.

Nevertheless I digress. I said I was going to talk to you about my children today. My son's name is Jace. I mentioned to you before that he's a soccer star. He started in soccer when he was four. He brought home his first trophy when he was six. It was for scoring the most goals. He came home and showed me with his little eyes shining so bright with happiness "Mommy, mommy, mommy, look what I did!" He jumped up in my arms and hugged me. It was little memories like that which kept me strong.

What they fail to understand in here is that a mother's love for her children can keep you strong in any light. They think that if you stay strong in here that means that you're evil, so they are harder on you. They torture you; don't feed you for days at a time, or when they do they lace it with tranqs to keep you subdued. The guards like to have it easy. The less they hear you the easier it is for the shift they work. The more subdued you are the less problems they think they will have. You learn what to eat and what not to eat. Stupidly they think I like applesauce. I don't. I eat a muffin or biscuit to put something in me but that's about it. They haven't been drugged.

Insane right? A drugged prisoner so you can have a peaceful night at work. Don't prisoners have rights, or at least deserve to be treated sort of humanly in here? Or is that depending on how severe they say your crime is.

The guard walked past and stopped when he was at my door. When he looked in the slot he commented that I should confess my crimes and not try to remember my life because that was over and I should thank god every day that I was at least allowed my shoe box cell. He then said I deserved less when they brought me here. Mind you, this guard and I are besties; super close friends. Ok that was my attempt at sarcasm. How'd I do? Yea probably not the greatest attempt but it made me feel good. I think that was a smile. I haven't done that in a while. I haven't done a lot of things in a while; like go for a run, go for a cup of coffee with friends, or even take a hot shower and soak the water into my skin. That sweet pure bliss of relaxation as the water hits your skin and washes away anything and everything.

Enough of that let me talk to you about my children. My son, when he got older, continued in soccer. I do wonder if he is now, or if he was, traumatized when I left that he didn't have his cheering section at all the games. I was so loud and proud. Every game I made sure I was there. It didn't matter to me if I had to work I always scheduled all the time off and made sure I was there for him. I think my boss hated me, but loved Jace and seeing him smile. When his mom was cheering him on he smiled and did well. I wasn't one of those parents that threw money at their kids to get them enrolled in something to keep them out of my hair. I was a very hands on parent. Even with my daughter. Let me tell you about her as well today.

My daughter, Grace. Yes, my children's names rhyme. So what, it's not like you can change them now. Wait what if their father had? To hide their public shame maybe. I hope they felt no shame from me. I hope that they knew I was innocent. I hope that their father stood up for me and told them the truth that I was taken for something that I didn't do. I worry about that every day. It's a wonder I'm not losing my hair with everything I worry about. It amazes me that I still have all of it. The only sign of the worry is a full shock of grey that's in there.

My daughter Grace was so beautiful and so smart. We always stayed up late at the end of the day talking and bonding. Even if we were prepping her for a test we did it together. She was in all Advanced Placement classes. The last test I helped her with was Math and she was correcting my answers. Math was never my strong suit. I was more History and Art. My son excelled in Science and English. They were both so smart. I think I've rattled your ears enough today. I am tired and I wrote a lot. Good night.

Day Four

The dreams came back last night. I was so tired after writing to you that I must have drifted into a deep sleep. Oh that's right I never told you about the dreams before. Sometimes they show me my childhood or when I met my husband and sometimes they show me things that I can't explain because they don't even make sense to me yet. I see visions in my head that look like a movie, but, it's me playing the parts. I don't get it. I should probably hide this page because I'm sure they will think that it's me saying that I'm guilty.

I just want to go back to my family and curl up with my children and never stop hugging them. When I was six I got close to a Rembrandt, within just enough room to touch it. The guard was so mad; she yelled at my parents and told them that if I didn't behave they would be asked to leave. She threatened that I would never be allowed back. I didn't know any better. I was six. My parents later told me that the guard was the type that thought children should be seen and not heard. I didn't understand it when I was younger but I made sure that when my children spoke they were always listened to within reason. They respected that.

But back to my mom and dad (I trail off way too much) my mother, when she dressed me as a child, always dressed me in soft colors and tones. She believed that surrounding a child in soft tones when they were young kept them calm and happy. It never made sense to me until I tried it with my own daughter when she was young. Sure enough, she was right. Amazing what our parents teach us that work well on our own young. There are times I wonder if my mother had taught me more, but I can't see it in my head. It's just one big blur.

Today the guard told me that they're keeping me in confinement. He said it was because I claim that I don't remember. Because I'm that dangerous. He told me I went into a building with Glock 9's that were loaded with 100 round clips in each hand which took everyone in there out. The death count total was 75 people. He told me that afterwards I robbed the place. A grand total of 2 million dollars went missing. They brought me in and tortured me and when I tell you tortured, I stop writing for a second to look down my shirt to see my scars, yea I have scars from when they first brought me here. You know that thing they call water boarding? Getting the shit beaten out of you? Then getting attached to a machine and have thousands of shock volts sent thru your body? Just to get you to tell the truth and all you can tell them is I don't know. Yea I'm that girl. They couldn't get out of me where the money was because I didn't know.

I'm still in astonishment. Me? I did that? I had to have my husband kill spiders for me, I'm completely failing at the moment to understand why, how, who, they think I really am. They showed me pictures of a woman who was my shape and size and I am skinny mind you. Skinnier now that I have been subjected to the gruel that this hell hole serves; but I am skinny nonetheless. I don't like violence it makes me ill. I don't seem to grasp how they connect me with this. Me! I was an Honor student for fuck's sake, a cheer leader, and a ballerina when I was younger.

There was a bombing in south Asia I was said to have been connected to as well. There were 3 buildings that were destroyed. The body count totaled 175 lives were taken from the 3 buildings. They said that the motive behind it was because the demands weren't met. 100 million dollars was the amount demanded. When the terms weren't met, building one was bombed. The bomber gave an hour to have the demands met adding 20 million dollars to the total. Again the hour passed with no payment. Building 2 exploded. The bomber upped the demands 5 million more. Thirty minutes passed and only 20 million was transferred. 30 more minutes passed. The bomber set off the final bomb. When the building fell the bomber sent an email from a roving ISP telling the embassy that because the demands were not met in full the final building fell. The guards and the pyscho, I mean the shrink bitch, yea you get the idea, I don't like her, started to spread clipping after clipping in front of me. My hands were clamped down in electronic cuffs so I couldn't push the papers away from me. The site of those children's bodies made me gag. There was not a bucket to puke in so I had to wait until they brought me back here. I puked this evening a lot I couldn't keep anything that was in my stomach down.

Afterwards, I crawled into bed to write to you. My thoughts are so scattered. I think that sleep is in order tonight. It's almost 3 am. The slave drivers will be buzzing the wake up sounds in 2 hours. Not that it does me any good I don't get out of this 6 x 9 hell hole. Wait... tomorrow is shower day. Maybe the overweight guard won't hit me while she watches me shower this time. She's so crude. The most (and yes, I'm a priss) deplorable comments have been said by her. I turned to her and told her I'm straight and she needed to leave me alone. She took my comment and made sure that I ended up with no food for three days. The thing, yes I called her a thing, told me it would be useless to complain. The warden hoped that I would rot in my cell. Great vote of confidence right?

When I came here the warden told me to keep my head down and mouth shut, which I've done, but nothing was said about not standing up for myself when it came to someone being abusive. A week later after my food punishment, the guards escorted me to the wardens office. When I sat down she asked me why I hadn't eaten. I asked if she and I could speak freely, without the guard present, since my hands were shackled to where I couldn't move. She obliged. The guard left. In attempts to overhear she left the door cracked. I remained silent. When the warden looked up she saw that the door was cracked. She got up and closed it herself after she reprimanded the guard for being nosey. She had told the guard that if she were to have a private conversation with a prisoner, private is private. More so, when it comes to the health and welfare of all the inmates even though some of us deserved to be fried in the chair rather than allowed our 6 x9 shoe box rooms and bedding to sleep on. But, a private conversation is a private conversation. It wasn't for their ears to have it be used against a prisoner later. Yes, she was aware that it was happening and it would stop now. She then turned on her heel moved out of the doorway enough to close it loudly. I smiled to myself quickly and erased it from my face before she sat down. Now why didn't you eat? I told her it wasn't that I didn't want to eat it was the fact that I wasn't given food. Why? Your plates were returned to the kitchen untouched. I told her about the shower incident. I then told her that I was appalled because I was very straight. I didn't have a problem with people of other preferences but long as they didn't direct them at me. Because I had shot her down and told her to leave me alone she took my food away. The warden then got really quiet for about 15 minutes and didn't say anything. I didn't prod her for anything either. She asked me if I hoped to gain anything from this. I said no. I reminded her of what she told me when I got here and said I had adhered to it. She nodded in agreement as this was our second face to face ever. The first was when I was brought in here. She had not had a reason to see me since.

She asked me about the charges and if I was going to admit to myself and her that I was truly guilty. I looked up at her in the eyes and told her I wasn't guilty. She shook her head with sad eyes. She then said that she wished I would remember everything. I looked at her blankly and told her that I was trying to remember my family. She changed the subject when she realized that she wasn't going to get anywhere with me. She asked if I was hungry. I told her no that I recently had eaten and was ok. She told me she was going to have the guard come back in and take me back. I nodded in understanding. She told me that she didn't want to see me back here. I nodded again. She then said before she called the guard back in that it was against the rules for them to withhold my food even if I denied them sexual favors.

She got up and had the guard come back in. she forewarned the guard that on the way back to my cell she would be watching and listening. She then told us that she didn't play favorites. She also didn't play that she was ok with guards playing games with her prisoners because that was her ass on the line and no one was going to place her ass in front of the firing squad. She had been in charge of the facility for 25 years and never had a casualty. She intended to keep it that way. She then excused me and told the guard to take me back. Her final words as we were walking out the door were, 'I might not like you, you're more than likely guilty, but this is my house, and until sentenced, or moved, or you die of natural causes, there will be no changes in how you are treated whether the guards here like it or not. It would serve you guards a lesson to remember that. This is my house and you are allowed to stay here because I allow it. That can change at any point if I so choose.

I went on more and now the alarm is going off for me to get up. I don't know why I don't get to leave here. Might as well get ready for shower. It will be nice to not smell myself for a day. I'm a priss, yes, I mind when I smell bad, and they don't give us deodorant because they are afraid that we will swallow it to make ourselves sick. Who knows? If I'm not too tired tonight I'll write to you and talk to you more. This is going to be a long day I can feel it.

#

Everything hurts from staying up so long. This is going to be a short entry today. It's nice to smell better. That's the only highlight of my day. I do remember when the highlights where my husband bought me a new pair of shoes or paid for a spa day. Good night I must rest now.

#

I was talking to you two days ago about the guard and no food and the warden. Yes I know you're paper and you know this already. What I didn't tell you was what happened after the guard brought me back. She whispered quietly, "Rat!" I kept my expression the same and made no sound. The guard brought me into my cell and released my shackles. When she walked back towards the door she turned and looked at me and stared. It was a warning stare. Feeling slightly brave I pointed at the camera that was above my door on both sides reminding them that they could be seen and heard. The guard shut the door and secured it. I smiled.

Maybe they will finally leave me alone and let me be in peace while I'm here. That request was personal and not ever voiced nor granted. They left my food alone. But they found ways to torture me. Snide comments and having to wait until all of the other prisoners had showered so all the hot water was gone. Cold showers really aren't fun but when you need to wash and smell better you suck it up and show no fear in here. They will smell it and own you that's all I have for tonight. Good night.

Day Seven

You know I've been sleeping better since I started writing to you. Well, minus the nights that they give me shock therapy. But, yes, it seems as though you are conducive to my sleep patterns. There were no dreams last night, but, I suspect that they will give me shock therapy again soon to try and make me remember. They tried once putting me under hypnosis. That was a total joke. I sat there and looked at the doctor the whole time and said are you done yet, because I can pinch myself without you telling me too?

They weren't very pleased about that. There are people in this world who aren't susceptible to hypnosis. I happen to be one of them. Too bad... so sad... It's scary to me that my attitude has become that way. I mean, wow, I never told my kids that ever. That was never a phrase that entered my mind. Not even once. Being here has made me cold and calculated. But, I've lost my carefree spirit, which hurts at times because I loved being free even though I am married.

Tomorrow I bet will be shock day. Which also means that the dreams will come back. I might have something new to tell you about. The dreams usually come back and maybe I will be able to make more sense of the ones I couldn't explain before. I'll tell you this, the dreams where dark and no place I ever want to see in reality. I feel like I need to call you my friend, but you're just a piece of paper. I don't know, but it's nice having someone to talk to that can't tell me that I'm a piece of shit, take my food, or talk back to me and say I need to just die because I'm scum who killed children. I think that's enough for tonight. Good night I will see you again tomorrow.

Day Eight

There was no shock treatment today which was a surprise. The guard said I was lucky. They also told me that they were lucky because they didn't want to half drag my body back to my cell afterward. Lazy asses. Oh crap, where did that come from? I'm so negative lately. It's more when the guards come through. They have such nasty tempers. I mean, I get that they have other people give them a hard time, but, for quiet people like me who don't give them shit and don't cause trouble, you would think that they would shut the hell up. They don't. They act stupid because they want to fill out negative reports to make your record look bad.

I told you a few days ago I paid heed to what the warden had told me. It's something I won't ever forget as long as I'm in here. Perhaps these guards find me stupid. I really don't care. I'm smarter than their games and I'm certainly not going to fall for it. I don't need my semi-spotless record blemished by someone who has fuel to burn. When they read this; when I get taken out of here for the next treatment, they will probably be pissed and show the warden but I don't care. Because then the warden would know what else that they do when she's not looking to get us written up. Those write ups keep us here longer. They add time to our sentences. Which I mean, if you ask me, it's essentially stupid because it comes out of the tax payers money. But what do I know? I'm just an inmate. I think that's all that there is for tonight. I really don't have a lot to add. It was really just an annoying day because these guards are morons.

Good night friend. I will talk to you again soon. Tomorrow, obviously, but that's beside the point. I must sleep now that I got all that off my chest. I feel better.

Day Nine

I am tired today. It was shock day. They set it at a lower volt because I had a few days off and they didn't want to fry my insides before they got a confession out of me. They hope that this will jolt me into remembering what I had done. I'm always so tired after them, and so thirsty. They make me wait to eat though. Evidently, after shock therapy, you will vomit and well I'm already skinny according to them. They didn't need to have a bulimic prisoner. Though I'm sure that they wouldn't mind if I was dead, they still followed some rules. Mind you, the food here is not yummy. You take a few bites to put something in your stomach to make it look like you have eaten and push the rest around so they see that you played with your food and ate a little bit. Everyone in here does it.

The guard was crass one night and asked me if the meals weren't gourmet enough for me since I claimed I was from a better background. I didn't claim anything. My husband and I traveled every year. So I had indeed eaten exotic foods from Spain and France. What I wouldn't give right now for a piece of real soda bread with fresh butter just out of the oven. We went to Ireland as well. My kids were well traveled. They came with us on all our trips.

Before they brought me here we were planning on spending two weeks in Greece. We always went as a family and enjoyed the culture and learning new things. My daughter loved the boys and shopping. She always said it was her way of learning the culture. My husband and I laughed. No matter how boy crazy she was, she always stopped by the end of the summer and was back to business when school started.

I'm done for today. Good night friend. I am wiped out from shock therapy today.

#

I don't think that I can explain last night. I went from telling you about my vacations and boy crazy daughter, to going to sleep and dreams of waking up going to boot camp and going to martial arts classes. I'm not that girl.

In my dream I flipped a grown man over my shoulder in sparring class. I don't understand that, or where it came from. My parents had never let me take those classes. They were hippies. They didn't condone violence. My mother had a heavy dislike for guns and hitting. She never hit me when I was in trouble. She preferred to talk it out and always just took something away from me. It was effective. It made me respect her and my possessions. It also made me think three times not to do something wrong. I really didn't like losing my music player. This dream just didn't make sense to me at all. I wish they would stop the shock therapy treatment and let me live in my bubble. They aren't going to release me, or at least that's how it appears, so why not let me be in my room, (this almost semi-existent little bubble of happiness) and let me be in peace? As the guard put it once, "Welcome to hell you're going to enjoy rotting here."

I guess they were right, but at least now I have you to talk to. Before it was no one and I was left to deal with this madness that is in my mind on my own. I sure can't talk to the bitch about it. My gratefulness to you at this time knows no bounds. Sometimes I wish that you were real so I could really talk to you rather than just write. Maybe I would sleep more soundly. I've always believed that when you verbally release something it is more effective and helps you relax once it's out in the open.

   This helps me open my mind but at times I wonder, too, if I even want to know what's next from these dreams. It feels mostly like you're holding my hand through the events of them but in a kind fashion, not in a barbaric 'you do everything wrong and are a sociopath' manner, that the bitch (I mean the shrink) does. I suspect that if you were real it would feel the same way, or maybe you would think I'm crazy too, like the rest of these people do. I have no idea, but, I do know that I'm going to take what I have right now and run with it. The almost thought that if you were real scares me and makes me want to crawl back into my shell and stop all this writing.

   No, I'm just being paranoid now. Maybe I was wishing for something and expecting the worst, so it would all blow up in my face. I almost wanted to ask the guard for a sedative, but I don't know what they would give me, or how long I would be out for the count. Tomorrow is therapy day. This is what they do; I have a day to rest after shock day so I don't sound or act too stupid. They take notes on all that stuff. They note erratic behaviors, like lab rats, confined to tight quarters. I need to stop this and head to bed. Otherwise it's going to be a long day tomorrow. I need to relax and sleep or she's going to find some way to torture me. She could try to hypnotize me again. That would be funny. Oh ok, I'm really just ranting now. I'm going to exhale deeply and attempt to pass out. Good night.

Day Eleven

Today was an epic day of cat and mouse with that woman. She has the nastiest habit of talking down to people, and making them feel like specs of dirt. She doesn't seem to understand that isn't how you get people to open up. That's how you get them to revert back into the hole in which you want them to crawl out of. But, I'm no psychotherapist, so what do I know?

I did dream again last night. But, I didn't dare tell her about it. I keep what is told to her fluffy, pink, and pretty. Which is what I think annoys her most about me. The hypnosis doesn't work; she can't get deep inside my mind to find out what my triggers are and what sets me off. I do like that sessions with her are the one thing that I can remain in control of in spite of the shock treatments to loosen me up. Stupid people. It's like there's a person inside me screaming out at you, 'I'll never tell, I'll never tell.' Don't ask me why I feel like that, but I do. I swear I have a headache after her sessions. Isn't she supposed to be calming? I feel more relaxed after I talk to you at night. I need to ask for a new marker to write with. This one is getting low. So if you don't hear from me for a few days it's because the guard said no. It really shouldn't be up to them, but they like to feel high and mighty. So telling you that having that is a privilege and you haven't behaved enough for their liking...You haven't kissed ass enough is more like it. So you don't get to have privileges. It's stupid if you ask me. The guards who get off on seeing what girls will give up. Sexual favors for extra privileges. Yes I'm locked up in this hell hole and I will tell you now that the guards are hateful, spiteful, derogatory, self-absorbed, assholes. Wow where did that come from?

I feel so bipolar sometimes talking to you. Again like I told you the other day I'm glad you can't talk back. Not like her. You can tell her how you feel and she tells you that you shouldn't feel like that because you're in prison. You should feel thankful that they haven't offered you your last meal and dosed you with something to never wake up again. I'm thankful for that. I'm also thankful that I still remember my children. She asked me what kind of contract killer wants or has children, or even has any regard for anyone other than themselves. She replied for me; there was none because that would make me a complete sociopath. Which she then followed up with saying that she knew I was one anyway. I was a complete piece of trash to have committed all those murders. They should have fried me when they brought me here.

I asked her if she talked to her own children like that. She looked so cross and said I was insubordinate. She told me that she would make sure that the volts here turned up higher for my next treatment. That way she could hear me scream the way everyone I killed screamed when they died. Maybe that would teach me to think twice before I was insolent. She laughed when I just looked at her. I finally told her if you need to feel powerful and inflict torture please go right ahead. You record our sessions and you can tell when something is deleted or modified and you have to keep all records of our contact. So please if that will make you feel better go ahead. It's your medical license on the line, not mine. She wasn't pleased that I stood up for myself. It gave her less power over me, which is not what she wanted. She wanted me to fear her like everyone else did. That wasn't going to happen, not now, not today, not ever. She wouldn't get that reaction from me, nor would she have the luxury of seeing me fear her.

I think I've ranted enough about her today. I have one more day until shock day and then the cycle starts all over again. I hope I sleep soundly tonight. I don't want to go to dream land again. I just want to go past REM sleep and stay there until it's time to get up, but that won't happen. Good night.

23

Day Twelve

I had a hard time after I said good night. It was a real bitch to fall asleep. The guard came in the morning and said that shock days were to be bumped up to twice a week now. The doctor's orders he said. I wonder if I should complain to the warden. She would probably tell me that I should have minded my tongue. I just don't understand why I have to mind my tongue when someone's being abusive. Do they talk like that to us because we're convicted, and we need to be treated a certain way to make us feel some form of remorse?

Yes, I still tell you that I'm not guilty. I'll hold to that until the day they set me free, or the day I die in here. I asked if I could talk to a lawyer and they laughed. Why would I want to talk to a lawyer? Because I wanted to know how my DNA matched what little they found in the crime scenes, I wanted to read my file, I wanted to see what cards were stacked against me. They kept telling me no and after months, and months of being told no, I finally gave up. It's sad they wouldn't even let me see a public defender. They said that no one in their right mind would hear my case. So why be stupid and make more of an ass of myself than I already have? When I questioned why they hadn't let me go to the first trial, I was told it was an open and shut case. When I asked why I wasn't put on the stand so I could defend myself; they said that I couldn't stop screaming so they had to drug me and sedate me. That was the only way to keep me quiet and calm. I asked why I was screaming and they told me I was screaming over and over again that I was innocent. I would tire myself out by screaming in the beginning only to wake up and start screaming all over again, which was when they implemented the drugs and dosing me. That makes sense to whom? Not me, but they think they know what's best here. There was one morning when I woke up just lying there in a catatonic like state. I didn't eat or drink anything. I didn't move. I just laid there in the fetal position, with my eyes wide open. They tell me that's how I look after shock therapy as well. I am a lump that needs to be carried back and dropped on my bed. Nice, right?

Let me tell you more about yesterday with my BFF. I think I'll call her that from now on. No, it's fake, and I can't do that. She's fake, and I am not. Ok, I'll start over. Let me tell you more about the shrink bitch. Yes, that's a better name for her. She said she wanted to make me scream the way everyone else had when they burned to death in the bombings. I almost wonder if she's trying to scare me. We shall see. I've told you quite a bit; I know I've told you quite a bit tonight that things are starting to come back to me as I sit here and un-file them and write them out to you on paper. As I've told you before I still think you would tell me that I'm insane but I'm trying really hard not to indulge that thought. You have simply become someone who I can talk to who doesn't point fingers.

Back to her... she told me yesterday that I should forget about my children because they have forgotten about me. They wouldn't need to remember a killer for a mother. I was a monster. I was no mother, and I was a disgrace to think that I could call myself one. I should remember that. I wasn't worth the word. She's a real head case. I mean I see a wedding ring on her finger but was she happily married or was her husband cheating on her? Or was she cheating on him? Maybe she was a lesbian, or maybe the ring was a prop, so she could feel better about herself when she was in here talking to us like we're beneath her? Maybe some of us are. There's a woman in here that opened fire on a childcare center. And another who set fire to a men's clinic because her husband was cheating on her with another man. I pissed her off when I got here and started to come down off the drugs they doped me up with. Why they set me loose in the commons when I was coming down, I don't know. Stupid fucks. I asked her if she wasn't doing her wifely duties and keeping

25

her husband pleased in bed. Doing that landed me with a black eye and a swollen lip. Normally I'm not like that. I don't say mean things to people about their sexual preferences and pick on them. Those drugs did a number on me. I went to medical, and she went to solitary. The doctor laughed at me when he realized who I pissed off. He told me I was stupid. He hoped that from this, I didn't have a target on my backside. I didn't understand what he meant at the time until she tried to stab me. That was what landed me in here, and her still out there. Even though she could have landed in here, her minions could have still done something to me for her. She was stupid. But I'm safe and away from her. They could live in fear of her. The doctor laughed at me, and told me all in due time I would be like them and not like men anymore. You're in a women's facility. Your life as you knew it is now over. Male comforts as you know them are now done and over, unless you sleep with one of the guards. But that's highly not advisable. They sleep with anything and most of the girls that come in here are dirty and disease ridden. The guards share it with all the other girls because they become carriers. For what though? To have extra smokes? Extra rolls with dinner? More toilet paper? Maybe a knife so that they could threaten other cell mates with to gain some form of power? And then there are the less fortunate. Those are the ones that are raped, because their file said that they were a street walker, or they had committed murder and were small... or even an accessory to murder. The guards took advantage where they could. They had zero shame in it as well. They knew it was survival of the fittest. I think that's another reason I'm locked in here. My second month here, when I was able to still keep time, one guard tried something. They came into my cell and told me not to scream or he would make it worse. That was when I bit him. He screamed like a little bitch. It was loud enough to alert someone the guard was caught with his pants down. Thank god he didn't have a chance to get mine down so it looked like I had invited him to attack me, because I didn't. My husband was all I wanted, and that was all that there would ever be. Not some piece of shit guard, who had a constant boner, and the need for fresh meat.

You would think that in prison they would not want to screw everything that walks. Hell, I don't want diseases from anyone. I have a hard enough time with the fact that they're stingy with the showers. Why would I want to be dirty and disease ridden all together? I think that if I had been raped and left with a disease, I would have offed myself. Yes, perhaps that's the chicken's way out, but I don't think I would have been able to live with that.

It's late, and I've really ranted enough tonight. I'm going to head to bed. Shock day is tomorrow. Good night.

Day Thirteen

She cranked the volume during the shock treatments. I am so drained from today. I didn't even eat. I can barely hold my head up to talk to you. I mean write to you.

Day Fourteen

Wow, I passed out writing to you. I didn't even finish a full sentence. I just passed out with face planted in my pillow and marker still in hand. The dreams did return last night yet again. I wonder if it's because she cranked the volume so much, I was mentally and physically juiced from the day. The dreams came back last night. This time I was clad in black leather sitting in a cafe. My laptop was in front of me, while I was watching the screen for something. The words on the screen were completely illegible. I was smoking. I don't smoke. The phone buzzed in my dream as well. When I answered it, all I could hear was my voice saying it was done. The phone went silent and something blipped on the screen. I hit a key and then shut the computer down. I got up from the table and looked around before I packed up and walked out. I stopped on my way and looked at the sign in front of the cafe.

In my dream I couldn't read the words on it. Maybe it was to remember what was served there. I don't know. I lingered looking at the sign for a bit more. Then I left and walked down the road. After that little bit, I woke up some. I had been asleep for about an hour, maybe an hour and a half. I just lay there trying to make sense of it all. When I dozed back off, I went to a different place. This time, I was standing in a hotel room at a window watching something through binoculars. What, I couldn't tell you, but man as I watched myself, I looked like a peeping tom. My hair at the time was short and red. I do not look good as a red head. I was clad in black, like a spy. What was I supposed to be looking at? I could see myself and what I was doing, but nothing more on the other side, or what, or who I was waiting for. There was nothing.

I didn't dare tell any of this to the shrink today. She would have had a field day with all of it, and picked through everything one by one, then proceed to tell me I was a liar. Today when I was with the bitch; yes you have figured out that I call her that. Well, not aloud I don't, but to myself. I just sat there quietly, and let her drone on. She tried hard to egg me on about the shock therapy. It didn't work out how she wanted it to, but then again she's not very bright in the art of egging people on. Her tone totally changes, and I was tired and not receptive to it at all, which helped me in the long run. "How did it feel?" she asked, "When the volts were going through you." You would think that it would have sunk in before, when she asked me why I hadn't slept because I looked overtired to her. I slept I told her, and said nothing more. She tried one more time to prod me. To which I turned it around and said maybe I would be more energetic if I was allowed to go out and exercise in the yard. Perhaps fresh air would help. Maybe I would sleep better so I wouldn't look so tired to her. Who the fuck was I kidding? They weren't going to let me out, she laughed. She thought I was being silly. I suppose her response to that was she would see if the warden would approve it. She added that it would be highly unlikely that they would have the man power to pull for a request like that. I guess then you're wondering why she was saying no, but supposedly it takes a lot of man power to have guards stand while I exercised, solely because she worried about my health while others were out there. No, she didn't worry about others because of how shackled down I was. She wasn't concerned. The bitch was morally corrupted. I'm sure, with everything I have in me, that she wouldn't bat an eyelash if I was killed in my sleep tonight. She might only be moderately irate, because she couldn't have watched me scream. She's like a modern day, but female, Dr. Jekyll.

Women are sick creatures. They say men are, but really women take the cake on certain things. I mean, who the hell gets off on basic electrocution or watching someone be electrocuted? A sick fuck...that's who. When she ended the session she asked if I wanted something to bite down on. I didn't reply. She's probably going to ask me again tomorrow as well. Sadistic bitch.

I went back to my cell and lay down. The guard thought it would be funny to tell me that if I was too tired he could make sure that I wouldn't be bothered when dinner was brought through. I laughed softly when he said that, and told him that they were still monitoring my food, so it wouldn't be in his best interest to make sure that the food didn't come to my cell. The warden would question it. He called me a stupid bitch and opened the door to my cell. I walked in and sat down on the bed. He didn't follow to undo the shackles. He just shut the door behind him and left. I said nothing. He wouldn't be my guard in the morning. You're asking how I'm writing this if I'm cuffed. I've learned to become skilled in twisting my hands. If I tried hard enough, I could get the shackles off I'm sure. These were just the metal kind, with a key that opens them. The electronic ones I wouldn't be able to wriggle out of without setting off an alarm.

Sneaky bastards if you ask me, but they should know their guards are assholes, and like to play games with the prisoners. That's all I have for the night. I'm going to eat, and hopefully pass the fuck out. Good night

Day Fifteen

Yesterday and today seemed to both roll into one. I didn't really sleep well before they took me back in for shock therapy again. However, in my tired state, there was an amusement to be found. I just lay there quietly and took it, much to her dismay. When she cranked the volume, up I didn't utter a word or make a sound. I just continued to lie there quietly. This bitch is not going to own me. She's not going to have the satisfaction of watching me scream out, even though my insides want to tear themselves apart. Every time she raised the voltage, my skin feels like its on fire, my finger nails felt like they were separating, and my hair follicles literally felt deader than they already were. My bones ached and went slack when she cranked the voltage one final time. I'm sure she was expecting me to scream. Instead I passed out. I'm sure she was thrilled about it. They brought me back to my cell while I was passed out. For once I didn't have to hear those assholes run their mouths about how degrading it was for them to have to carry a grown adult back to their cell. Small reprieve, yes? I thought so too. That's why I'm awake and talking to you, rather than telling you that I am too tired to talk to you tonight. I'm not quite sure what they hope to accomplish by picking into my brain. They might find that I have a deep desire to paint and a love for music. Perhaps they would uncover that I was saving for a pair of Louboutins. Who knows? Would they maybe even make me tell that I had an account saved up for a real Louis bag? I'd been saving for two years. All the extra savings from couponing the market runs. He would have laughed at my silly behavior. How did he think we were able to afford all those trips? I mean I love my husband dearly, but at times he was daft when it came to how much I saved so we could have the finer things in life. My daughter had label jeans that came from discount stores and school bags that normally cost $50 and up, I got for $20. She was always pleased. My son had new gear for sports. His friend's parents always made them re-use things. I saved and pinched pennies from one place to put it in another. That seems stupid that she would want to get in my mind for that. Maybe she wants to know about the secret dreams that I've entrusted you with. They would probably think that it is senseless and stupid nonsense. That I was being delusional, which I feel like I am being when I have those dreams. It feels like another lifetime. It feels that I was another person who is completely taken over. I just don't understand it. It makes no sense what so ever. Could that make me crazy? I'm sitting here trying to figure out what they want from me. That shouldn't make me crazy. That should make me wonder if they're crazy. Maybe the next time I'm in the bitch's office, I'll ask her how long I've been locked up here. That should really make for an interesting conversation, since I really have no concept of how long I've been here. She might say that it's beside the point. Who knows? Why can't I remember things like that? Why can't I understand what the hell these dreams mean? It's like looking at my life from a mirror, and I don't get it. It makes no sense in my head and I really want it to make sense. I want it like you have no idea. Maybe it would help me sleep at night. The only thing that seems to help right now is this writing to a non-existent person.

Day Sixteen

These last three days have blended together. I hope I sleep some. I did have a dream last night. I was in the shower. It was a square shower in the middle of the stone tile room. The nozzle and the water pipe were suspended from the ceiling, and there were four attachments from the pipe that allowed for rods to be connected for a shower curtain to hang down, which one did. It was clear so you could see inside it. Looking at myself from the outside in, you could see I was covered in blood. As I sat on the floor in the middle of the shower, just letting the water hit me while blood washed off and went down the drain. The expression on my face was that of calm. There was no panic. Why wasn't I panicking with all that blood? What the hell was wrong with me? It was like I was calmed by watching the blood. There should be nothing in anyone's right mind about seeing blood that should calm. I re-read what I just wrote to you and it still makes no sense. What was I doing in that shower? How had I gotten covered in blood? I watched myself in the shower while I sat there. I finally got up and grabbed the soap, and cleaned myself and washed my short hair. The suds went down the drain along with the pink blood stained water. I stood in there under the water until it flowed clearly. Only after that did I hop out and turn off the valves and step out of the clear curtains onto the tile.

I watched myself grab a towel from the hook on the wall. Watching more, I saw myself walk on the tile floor in the nude, like it was nothing. Personally, I am a pansy when it comes to cold floors and wet feet. It just makes it colder. But, I'm watching a version of myself in this dream I'm telling you about, which the

34

opposite of what I know of myself and really doesn't add up. But nevertheless in this dream, I covered myself in the huge white towel, and dried my hair off with a smaller towel.

After I was done I went into another room and found a small closet with slacks and sweaters. They were all the same cut and style, and were hanging. I pulled them off the hangers and put them on. In that room, there was a table with a chair. The table was set up with a laptop and a phone, which I watched light up when I was finished dressing. I watched myself pick it up and answer in Russian. I don't speak Russian, so I can't tell you what was said. But I did write something down, and then clicked the phone off and closed the laptop. Following that I disconnected the cables, and tucked them into a nearby pack. There was a laptop case that fit into the pack. Everything was bundled up in speedy fashion as I watched along. I went back to the closet after, and took out a pair of boots meant for biking, quickly put them on, and laced them up. I gathered everything up, and then went outside in to the hallway grabbing a leather jacket and a set of keys. There was a main door. I went to it. I Opened and shut the door behind me. I woke up in a pool of sweat after that.

That was the longest, clearest dream I've had. I don't understand it a bit. Again though, if I tell anyone, they will think I'm crazy. They already do in here anyhow. But, whatever I'm locked up for, no way am I going to add to whatever they already charged me with. I don't think I care anymore. I think I've rattled your ear off enough. I need sleep. Good night.

Day Seventeen

It's morning. I haven't been out yet to my sessions. I really want to know where the hell that building was. The one from my dream I told you about. Why can't I remember all of this? It's like so real and I can touch it almost, and touch myself while I'm in there. This has to be real. I can tell you that I'm not on drugs. I mean I wouldn't be if I could be, but that would explain the delusion. It would explain all of it. The dreams would have been drug induced. I don't know how to explain anything I've told you thus far. Just what's happened with the bitch. They will be coming soon to pick me up for head shrinking. I need to hide these papers.

Day Eighteen

I woke up from a dream last night in a sweat again. This time I was on the rifle range. It wasn't pretty. There were moving targets that I had to shoot. The fucking instructor was screaming at me "Finish this! Kill! Shoot or be shot!"

"Why do I need to kill them? It's plastic!!"

"Do it now! If you don't complete this course, you will end up in the hole for two months!! You're a maggot!! You don't get to feel!! You will do as you're told!! You're lucky to be here!! We could have killed you!! We should have left you for dead, you were a stringy haired coke addict!! You were laying there with blood dripping out of your coked out nose, barely fucking breathing, when the den you were whoring out in was raided! Get up and shoot or I will put you back in the hole, and find a way to end you!! Do you want to go back to having dried blood caked up and crusted around your nose?"

I guess for some reason I didn't like what I was being told, because I got up, pulled the trigger, and destroyed the targets.

What the hell was the hole? Why the fuck was I scared of it? I don't understand. I think I need a new shrink. I think I'd make this bitch run to the crazy house with all the things that are running through my head now. I'd love to drive that fucking whore to the loony bin. I mean the real loony bin, for the special kind of crazy that she already is.

Day Nineteen

Why can't I remember my sorority sisters? I think of them or I did think of them daily when I first came here. There was a basket that they gave the girls when they first pledged with mascaras, nail polishes, gloss, and so forth... I remember going back to my room and going through the basket, but that's it. I can't remember when I pledged. I can't see the things that should have happened during hell week. I can't see the stunts they make girls do. Why? I know it was there. I was there. This is insane. I need to be able to remember those things.

I remember everything.

They half dragged me back to my cell. I was crying while they dragged me. The shock therapy had been enough to make a grown man cry. The guard brought me back to the cell door opened it with his key pass and shoved me in. "There you go lump. It's not in my job detail to treat you nicely or put you in a chair or your cot." That was all he said before he slammed the door shut to lock my cell from the outside. My thoughts were scattered. At the most I could hope for karma fucking him in the ass for all the mistreatment he dealt out to people. I laid there on the floor where I had landed for about an hour or what felt like an hour. I looked up and finally saw there was a cup of water on the table. It was full and warm. I didn't like ice water after shock therapy my system didn't process it well and I usually puked. I struggled to get to my knees. I stayed there for about 15 minutes while I waited for the strength to grab on to something to bring myself to a standing position. I would shuffle to the desk table in my cell to get to the water once I could stand. There was a chair there that I could sit on or easily fall onto the cot that I slept on every night. No matter what this was going to hurt. I just kept telling myself I was going to make it. I reached out for the wall to start lifting myself up. My legs cramped up as I pulled up. My hands and arms felt like jello but I gripped hard and pulled.

I screamed silently and pulled myself up more. I cannot fall. I cannot make noise. There are guards that walk these halls waiting to hear something that happens in these rooms that isn't supposed to. Falling is failure and my story will be told. I don't know what happened. There were a lot of memories that were triggered. I needed water. I needed my marker and paper so I could write things down. The things I write down begin to make sense when I re read them. I pulled up again. Success. I leaned against the wall. There were about seven minutes that passed while I caught my breath. This was more than i expected to knock the wind out of me. It was time to shuffle to the desk. One foot in front of the other Rosie girl. You can make it there and sit down. I'm in my late 30's and all I can do is the granny shuffle. I had cat like reflexes once. There were a few flashes of things that went by my eyes. Memories of a life I knew. Everything else that was there slowly started to fade away. It was gone. Someone had programmed some of the things in my head. Other things were real. The kids were real. They weren't my blood but I did have days with them. I was placed in the home to keep an eye on the father. My husband, the marriage, had been a piece of paper and to someone it was an 'op.'

I remember everything. A few more shuffles and I would be at the desk. I just needed to push myself off of the wall. I pushed my hands near my boney ass. One, two, three, push Rose. I count out loud mind you. Yes i know it's childlike but I never really had a chance to grow up and become an adult. You see my hell began at a very young age. Where though? Ok Rosie one more time. One, two, three, push. I was off the wall. One foot in front of the other Rosie. Let's go. You're stronger than this. Let's go. Move. One foot in front went out and the other shuffled right along behind it. A few more paces Rosie you're almost there. I was telling myself this, not talking out loud mind you. Two more steps Rosie you're almost there. You can sit down when you get there. One foot went out and the other foot followed. The chair was in reach. You may think this was a big cell, but it wasn't. Four steps took a very long time when everything inside you burned. Your bones are stiff and sore Rosie. Everything screamed. The chair. I reached out gingerly for it wrapped my fingers around the top of the chair stretching my hands out and wrapping them around the chair like that was a hardship. The joints in my fingers screamed for help but my brain didn't respond. Just keep moving Rosie you can do this. Overcome the pain just like you have a hundred times before. Turn it off. One foot in front of the other Rose, get around the chair. You can sit down Fuck, I came close to breaking a toe. The leg of the chair came with so close to my pinky toe catching and breaking. There was another silent scream in my head. Don't make a sound Rosie. They'll come back in. They think you don't have any energy left. You shouldn't be up and running around after shock therapy like this.

At least that's what happened all those times before. They checked on me before and I would lay there for hours. I remember a few months ago one of the guards came in and kicked me to make sure I was still alive. When I screamed, he jumped. He was a stupid fuck. He was fired for what he did. He had broken a rib. He called me a cunt. The rib cost him. I was a liar he yelled. There wasn't anything in the room strong enough for me to break my rib on. Piece of shit.

There the chair was behind my ass now. I could plop down. As much as I wanted to lower myself into the chair slowly i fell into it and it hurt. Maybe if I had an ass to cushion the fall it wouldn't have hurt as much but it did. Don't scream Rose. You want to. Don't make a sound. They will hear it and come in. Don't say or make a sound. I waited a few moments until the pain died down. Water. What took me a half hour to get there was worth it. The water would hopefully make the burning joints stop. Maybe for just a little. I was extending my arm like after I had a blood draw. My veins were tender and screaming for sugar from all the nutrients that the blood sucker had just ass raped me of. There was no way I would fail. I drank more water. The cup was almost empty. I put my head down on the desk. I needed to rest for just a few moments. There were so many thoughts that were racing through my head. It was more than overwhelming. I didn't even know how to explain all the images I was seeing in my brain. I had a mother. I used to work at a pizza place when I was younger. I had a father too. He was a drunk. This didn't match up with anything I have written before. Why it was all coming back now? Maybe it was the shock therapy. I just needed to rest some. If I kept lying my head down or even on my cot just so everything didn't burn. No, that wouldn't work. I needed to get these thoughts out.

If I don't I'll forget them and the last little bit of time torturing myself will have been for nothing. Sit up Rose. I straightened up some. It was like I was a whole new person and one that was fighting back.

I am Rose. I was a good kid once. There were a lot of bad things that happened to me. Some choices, I made. Some choices were made for me. My marker. Yes I have my marker. There's paper. Put your hands out on the table Rose. Get the paper. The burning in my veins hurt to the point of wanting to scream again. Shut up Rose. You don't need to scream. They will come in if you scream and drug you, which will make you sleep and forget. Pick up the marker Rose. You need to write this down. I reached out again and began to write.

My name is Rose and this is my story.

Back In Time

Let me take you back in time to where my story begins. There was a time when I was a quiet kid. I didn't do anything to harm people. I was good and honest. I went to school. I had a job. I saved money. I even went to church now and then, though I don't think any of my prayer requests were ever answered. I sat in the back pew to not really be seen. There were too many busy bodies. People knew each other's business. Old women clucked in disapproval when they didn't see something. They clucked more when they saw something they didn't like. I laughed. Memories came pouring back in. whatever they did to make the abyss of my brain open up. It worked. I smiled at little things. I frowned at the larger that trickled in. I slammed my fist against the table when I saw the things I most regret.

There was no going back now. There was only forward. My name is Rose. I know I lost my way. I'm going to tell you the tale of how I became a cold blooded killer. What was ripped from me? A life that was once sad. What could have been described as warm and wonderful. I turn the page and begin my tale.

The Beginning

When I was younger I made the best of what we had. We weren't rich. My mama worked her hands to the bones to protect and raise me. There were nights where she had to leave me home when she worked a double shift. She worked so much only to come home to the idiot. She should have kicked him out and changed the locks but she never did. It was almost like she expected him to change or something but he never did. I never understood it. Maybe she thought he would change, but all the liquor did was fuel him up. He was always so violent with her. She always made me go in my room and lock the door. It was her way of keeping me safe. She didn't know it but I put a dresser in front of the door. That way if he came after me too, he would have a hard time getting through the door. It was an old oak dresser and it was heavy but on carpet floor it budged nicely for me and stopped where I needed it to go. It just worked. There were nights when he was done beating her he would try the handle. "Rose, open the fucking door, Rose. Rose I just want to talk to you." I pretended to be asleep. All the lights were out. Thankfully, there were no windows in my room since it was so close to the ground. It made my room cloudy and stale smelling from the cigarettes my mom gave me. A little bleach never hurt anyone. I washed my walls and so forth. My room was spotless.

She told me I could work after school. There were conditions. I had to be home before he got home. After dinner I had to clean up and make sure I was in my room before he got home. Her rules, I lived by them. She took the bruises he left on her for the both of us. I just never understood it until now. She wanted me safe

43

because I was her child. She took the abuse so I didn't have to. The bastard I called my father was 5'11 and broad shouldered. He wasn't fat or over weight but he was built. I remembered them saying he worked at a steel yard. She made better money. She was a paralegal during the day and waited tables at night. The tips weren't great, but it brought home gas money and that band tee shirt I really wanted. The extra things. It was nice when she and I went out we didn't get too often it was usually when he left and was on a three day bender and didn't come home. I never minded when he didn't come home. We got to be mother and daughter when he wasn't around, not mother hide my daughter because her fathers a pyscho. I don't get why he even came back after his benders. He needed to stay gone. The lazy bastard made decent pay and didn't do anything for us accept cause physical pain for my mother, and emotional pain for me, watching her deal with that asshole.

He never once hit her where the bruises could be seen. There were times where he cracked ribs. The skin was blackened and bruised underneath. She called off work for three days to get the swelling down. He left for two weeks that time. The morning after the swelling went down I got up to help her wrap her ribs up in a large ace bandage. It hurt me to see her bruised. It just made it easier to ignore him. I went to work I hid my checks. We went to the bank in the next town over to make an account in the local branch there. It was for me to go to college. But I never went to college. If she could see me now, she would have my ass in a sling of guilt. That kind of guilt that only one person can give you. Your mother. She told me always that I was a good daughter. She wished that she had given me a brother or sister. When she brushed my hair at night she was quick to retract that when he beat the shit out of her. No we couldn't be the Cleavers or the white picket fence family. I just have no good thoughts other than I failed her.

While I sit here in this cell and wallow in my thoughts of self-pity. I really should fast forward you more into my teens so you can see how much I have progressed from this. I'm being purely sarcastic, you need to realize. I didn't progress; I'll get to the icing on the cake later. Let me get back to the story at hand. There was a time where he was gone for a month. She got a gun; this was before there was a wait to buy them. You could walk into the store and show an ID and just buy them that day and take it home. She hid it in my room. She said it was for my protection in case he came back and it was also for me to protect myself if he ever made it into my room when the lights when out. She taught me how to pull it apart and clean it. She showed me how to load the clip and then she hid it under the floor boards near my bed, covered it with a rug and made me swear never to say a word to anyone about where it was or even if we had one. It was meant only for when things got so bad with him. She said the key word was red. When it was spoken it was time to act. She told me to do whatever it took to defend myself as well as defend her if I could, if she was still alive, after his attack. Maybe, just maybe, if I had been there she would still be alive. Why I reflect on this now 15 years later I don't know. Well it's because I missed her. She was my rock when I was young. I tried over the years to put that pain away deep into a part of me that I wanted to forget. I wanted to forget while all the bad was happening when I got older.

The night I had to use the gun was terrible. I was crying when the cops finally showed up. That night was awful. He came home earlier than usual. He was drunk and stumbling. She told me to go to my room and lock the door. That pissed him off and he slapped her hard. She fell and told me to run. "Go to your room and lock the door. Go, Rose, go." I just stood locked into place. She looked so helpless. I wanted to help her I just wanted to save her. I ran into my room and locked the door.

He yelled after me, "run, Rosie, run. You're worthless. You don't care about her. She's your mother." That angered me. Who was he to say I was worthless? I cared for her when he left her battered and bruised. I loved her when he didn't. I washed her tears away when she was sitting wishing and waiting and wondering how long it would be until he would return. She wanted him to love her again like when they first got together. She told me he was so gentle and caring. He wasn't anymore. He was a terror and I was pissed! I slammed and locked the door. I moved the rug and tried to pry the floor up I wasn't doing so well, my hands were trembling. When I got the floor board up I took it out. The gun was loaded with the clip in there. I loaded the barrel and made sure not to pinch my skin. I did that when she took me to the range to learn. It hurt and I had to keep my hand bandaged for a week after that. I put the floor board back and my rug as well and turned to unlock my door. There were no sounds outside my door so I knew he wasn't close. I carefully opened the door to where they couldn't hear me out there. I kicked off my shoes so he wouldn't hear me coming. I heard him smack her hard again she fell again. I turned the corner I saw he had a bottle of whiskey in his hand and was taking a drink off of it. He called her a slur of words most of what I couldn't understand, the liquor had taken over completely and his speech was shot. In a low voice I told him to get away from her. He stumbled when he turned around to look at me. He couldn't see the gun where I held it behind me. "What did you say to me little girl?" he slurred, "what did you say?"

I Shot Him

I just looked at him and said "back away from her slowly." My hands were behind my back I drew them out and aimed the gun at him. I don't know what I saw in his eyes when I aimed it at him. I think it was a mixture of fear and hate.

"What are you going to do Rosie? Shoot me? You're nothing but a scared little girl, Rosie. You don't know how to use a gun." He sneered after he said that. For a brief second there was silence. He looked at me like he was ready to lunge at me. I fired off a shot. It hit him. He staggered back, grabbed his shoulder, and screamed out in pain. My mother managed to scoot herself away from him on the ground while I had him distracted. She was safe so he didn't trip over her while he fumbled around after I shot him. I wanted to shoot him again to keep him from hurting us; from beating her more. He came forward again like he was going to try and lunge at me. I aimed for the foot and fired. He jumped when the bullet hit his foot. He screamed aloud like a little girl.

"You fucking little bitch, I'll kill you" he cried. Maybe it was the sheer fact that he pissed himself when I shot him the second time. Maybe that's why he was crying. Maybe he was in real pain. Who the hell knows?

I started screaming at him while he was crying. "You're a sick fuck, old man. You have terrorized us for years. You really thought that something wouldn't come back to bite you in the ass from this?" I remember I started to wonder if someone had called the cops finally. This reign of his terror would be over tonight. I had told myself that I would tell the cops everything. I would tell every last single thing about him and what he had done to us over the years. All the bruises he's left on my mother. The years of him telling me no one would believe me if I told them. Why would he leave bruises on a para legal? Who would believe that? Seems a little insane don't you think Rose? He would tell me this. "Rosie, who is going to believe a 16 year old girl? I hate to tell you this no one's going to believe you? You're no one Rose. You're just a kid, and Rose, if someone does believe you. I might go away for a little while. When I get back I'm going to beat her harder so you'll wish you had kept your mouth shut." I just looked at him in disbelief. How could someone be so cruel? I really should not ever have asked myself that. It's silly. I've known since he was five he was a dirt bag. That was the first time I had woken up to her crying. I walked out of the bedroom to see him standing over her.

I thought for a second that I heard a siren in the distance. I froze. Are they finally going to come here? I need this madness to end. Little did I know then it wouldn't end for a very long time. I looked at him. "You sorry son of a bitch you're going to jail tonight. Not a chance in hell you're going to go free. There's not a chance in hell that I'm going to let you harm her anymore. You're no man. You're nothing but a fucking piece of shit." He came at me like he wanted to slap me. I cocked the gun at him. I would shoot again if I had to.

She stopped me. "No Rose, don't. Just because he can walk doesn't mean he's not hurt from the other two shots you took at him. If you hurt him more you're going to get into more trouble. Do you hear the sirens Rose? Let them come take him away."

"Mama, I don't care anymore. I can't have him hurt you. His pleasure is in our pain. He doesn't care. He's sick. This is sick." I started to cry more.

The idiot screamed at us. My mother shut up. She was used to being quiet when he was loud. That made sure she wasn't going to be hit again. It was typical of him. Be loud. Shut women up. His face smiled. "You stupid bitch. You're weak." He was talking to my mother. "You're always going to bend to my will. That's all that's ever going to be. I'm always going to win." he smirked. "You little bitch. You won't save her. You won't even save yourself."

Arrested

They came. The cops. They took her statement and his. They asked me as well what happened, but I was a minor so I don't think they could really count what I was saying at the time. He told the cops I shot him. He was attacked by us both. I screamed that it was bullshit. The cop was male, they all were. I'm pretty sure that's illegal now, but then I guess they didn't care. Maybe it was easier. I heard him whimper to the cop that I was a horrible daughter. I stayed out until all hours with boys. The cop was more than happy to believe him. His daughter was the same way. I was a virgin his daughter was not. His daughter was in my class. She was a slut and all the boys knew it. Back to the cop. I screamed at him again and told him my lovely father came home on a regular basis drunk as a skunk. He beat her every time he came home like that. It was the nights he didn't come home we were lucky. When I was screaming at the cop I told him that he should call an ambulance to have her looked at for bruises and to make sure that nothing was broken. They just laughed. I screamed, "Are you fucking corrupt?"

That's when the asshole hobbled over to me and slapped me. "You shot me you little whore, after I gave you life and a roof over you and your mother's head. You shot me. What did I do to deserve this? I'm your father. You're ungrateful. You're a slut." He spat those words at me. My eyes widened. This man, who helped bring me into this world and the cops in this world were both equals. Low life leeches. I knew that already in the back of my mind. Why it came to me like that I have no idea. The cop didn't read me my rights. He sure did slap some cuffs on me. He and his partner escorted me out to the squad car. I fought a bit on the way

50

to the car. There were two of them, and it took the both of them to get me into the car.

The Squad Car

The ride to the station was at first quiet. They tried to get me to talk by making comments like the girls in jail were going to love me. When that didn't work they said I was a lesbian. Maybe they actually took me seriously when I was screaming at home that I was a virgin and I wasn't like his whore daughter. They started riding me more and more saying I was a lesbian and the girls were going to love me. That's when I started talking. "I don't care if I was attacked it would be on their heads if my mother was dead or harmed when I got out. You believed a drunk over sober people. You never had her checked. She's bruised, battered, and not just from tonight. He's been abusing her for years.

"There's never been a police report, Rosie," the cop replied. "All we know is you shot your dear old dad.

"Why do you think there were no reports? He's a psychopath. He threatened the neighbors. He told old Mrs. Lincoln on the corner he would burn her house down while she slept if she called the cops. Why do you think no one else said anything? He threatened all of them; he played the nice show husband for a while so people would think that there was nothing wrong. Maybe you don't want to see all that because you're male. Your gender is a bunch of sick fucking individuals. If it was you, and your mother was being abused by your father you would want help. Wouldn't you?"

"My father wouldn't beat or abuse me," the cop sneered.

"Of course he didn't you piece of shit." He looked back at me.

"You have a dirty mouth Rosie. What's say we fix that when we get you into lock up tonight. Maybe you'll learn some respect."

"My mother will come and bail me out."

"Not likely Rosie we are requesting you be held without bail. You're a danger to yourself and others. Perhaps the psych ward in a hospital would be good for you Rosie. That way you hear everyone scream at night like your dad screamed when you shot him. That would teach you a lesson wouldn't it?"

"No it wouldn't you fat fuck. It would just fuel the hate I already have in me for you. Mark my words you over grown nimrod. I will come for you if a hair on my mother's head is out of place. You left her there with the man I shot. He might be my sperm donor but he's no father of mine. You left her there in the line of his alcohol infused rage. He will keep coming for her until she's dead. Did he pay you off? Are you on the take? Do you think this is right?"

He finally got on his CB radio and called his dispatcher and told them that they would need restraints when they got to the precinct. They would also need a hypodermic needle filled with a tranquilizer to subdue me. He said preferably a Xanax or a Valium injection. If threatening won't work with her we'll just have to knock her ass out until her arraignment.

"Go ahead and drug me. The judge will know when they don't get the proper response from me. They're going to ask me what happened you fat fuck. I'm going to tell them that he was beating her and I defended her. I'm going to tell them you didn't have her checked out. You didn't even read me my rights when you cuffed me. You just took his side because he has a penis." We were close to the station. It was a long drive from my house, but I could tell we were close. There was a gas station with a big donut sign outside it. We passed an impound lot the car turned from what I could see we were going down a ramp into an underground lot. I'm guessing we were parking underneath the police station. I looked out the window and saw there were three people outside that were not in uniform and six additional officers. I had to wonder why there were 11 people to take one teenage girl into custody. There wasn't anyone who was going to come rescue me from this. My cuffs were on the cops got out of the squad car.

"She's here. Muller, take her in." Muller was a large female cop. "Subdue her if you have to. She's been screaming the whole way back." Muller came around she had a large partner with her as well. The man was 6'4. It was dark in the garage the lights were dim. I couldn't see his name tag too well. It didn't matter I was here.

Jail

My trial was seriously stupid if you ask me. First I was held in jail for two weeks with a 200 pound 19 year old bunk mate who smelled terrible and peed the bed (thankfully I had the top bunk.) The smell of the cell was horrid. I don't think they understood that I wanted to puke every morning from the stench when I woke up. After enough dry heaving they finally gave me a bucket of bleach water to clean the cell with and a mop. I made my cell mate strip her bed and wash the mattress down. After that I scrubbed the floors and chairs. She looked at me like I was crazy but I just told her if we were stuck together it needed to be clean. She just nodded quietly. Later, before dinner, she asked me what my name was. I told her it was Rose.

Her name was Cheyenne. She was in for theft. She told me it was for stealing because she needed to fill her sister's and brother's stomachs. Her parents did not feed them. They were foster kids. The parents took the money and spent it on themselves, not the children like they were supposed to. She told me the 'mom' had a powder habit and the dad was a drunk. It was odd to think that all the money they got landed up her nose or down his throat. When kids went back to their parents or adopted out to real homes or hit 18 they were terrible to them. She screamed that they were all costing them money. Cheyenne told me that since she had been there the longest, she knew better, she knew their house was paid off. She knew that there were grants for their water bills as well as their gas and electric.

When there was no food to eat Cheyenne went out to the store and started stealing small things. Little sleeves of donuts, to bring back to her foster siblings to eat. It wasn't much, and it sure wasn't healthy, but it put something in their stomachs to fill the pain so they could fall asleep. She told me it was the worst feeling ever watching the little ones go to bed with pains in their stomachs. When her foster parents caught on to what she was doing they gave her a choice she could keep feeding the kids but she had to start bringing home bigger things they wanted steaks. The choice was that she had to keep doing it or they would turn her in. They didn't get much money for her anyway since she was too old, or that's what they told her. The dad said she was too fat and no one would hire her for a job so she needed to keep stealing.

I stopped her to ask where her real parents were. She got very quiet. "Rose, my parents were in a gang, they were killed in a drive by." She just looked at me while I stared, like there was someone parents who actually did stuff like mine. Beat people up. I think she saw what I was thinking because she stopped me. "No, Rosie, my dad cherished my mom. He kept her safe even when the other gang members wanted to hurt her. Men don't respect women in gangs, but my dad respected his wife. She wasn't gang property. That's part of what got them killed. The other part that got them killed is they were in a cross fire... their gang and a rival. They were going to the market the two gangs opened fire and my parents were hit."

"When the cops came and got my baby sister and me they didn't tell us what happened. They didn't have a social worker with them which is what I've read is supposed to happen when you take minor children into custody. They took us to a social services place where we slept on cots for two days before someone came and talked to us. My sister didn't speak for two months after they died. She just sat there looking at the walls holding the last doll my parents gave her."

"Where's your sister now?"

"She was adopted out. We went to three different foster homes together. Then they split us up. For her it was a good thing. She was still young and she got adopted out to a good home. I don't think she knows I was arrested. I really hope she doesn't to be honest Rosie. I mean her big sister an overweight bed wetter. I'm sure even you don't think very highly of me for that either Rosie." I told her we all have problems. Mine was my dad. Now that I was away from him, it was the fear for my mom's safety. She nodded slowly.

"I can pray for you Rosie."

"Chy I can help you. We have a clock outside. If we cut your drinking off by 6:30 which is an hour before lights out, and like little kids if we make you go to the bathroom every 15 minutes it might help you. Do you want to try it?"

"Sure Rosie I mean, yeah, it's embarrassing. I think what triggers it is the fear of the fosters coming back into my life, but you want to help me and I feel calm around you."

"Chy, you set off my clean freak OCD, but, I like you. You're the first friend; the first real friend I have had since I was five, when my dad started beating my mom, and I knew it." They kept it rather hidden before that. He kept it to when I was sleeping. I slept harder when I was a baby. When I got older and anxiety kicked in, it made it harder for me to sleep. Chy told me maybe that's why I was so skinny. I had to laugh it was the first real laugh in a long time. We just sat for a while in our cell and didn't say a word. The officer on duty came through to make rounds. He told Cheyenne she should be careful. I was crazy. She just nodded and didn't say a word. The officer made a jab at her to me and asked if my dainty little nose was alright since it reeked of bleach in the cell. Rosie the shooter and Cheyenne the thief who pissed herself at night.

"Goading us will get you nowhere officer. Just be glad there's no cameras in here that record what you're doing. I'm sure you could lose your job harassing a minor much less two females. I don't think they'd look to highly on that do you officer?"

"Your mouth is going to get you in trouble Rosie."

"My name is Rose, officer, not Rosie. It would benefit you to remember that." The officer looked and laughed.

"Whatever you say little girl. It's your funeral in here remember that." The officer walked away laughing. Cheyenne told me not to worry about him he was all talk. I told her that after all the mess with my dad I didn't trust any man when it came to major or minor threats in here.

"Rosie I know, but, you have to control your temper. The attorney is coming from legal aid tomorrow like they told you earlier. You need to be calm so you can tell your side of the story. They won't listen to you if you're angry." I learned that the hard way. I was super angry at my public defender and mad at the world. "So just relax Rosie. I'll promise to keep my part of the bunk clean to so you don't stress out." I hugged her and we sat in silence for a while after that. A bit later we ate dinner and went to bed. The food was crap. I mean it was jail food so what did I expect even if I preferred a peanut butter and jelly sandwich? I suppose I didn't have a right to complain at least I was fed. She looked super embarrassed to go to the bathroom again like I suggested to her. I knew it would help her. We would just have to wait until the morning so I could prove myself right with the results.

When the morning came she almost cried for joy. "Thank you Rosie, I will be doing this from now on. I'm too old for this problem." It was six am and the guard hadn't come in to wake us up yet. It was quiet. We were the only two in this block since we were female and under twenty one. Cheyenne was not a minor but she still kind of was so they bunked her in here rather than with the 40 year old women who would have done terrible things to her. We were both hungry. It was six thirty am by the time we really started talking. She told me again that I needed to remain calm. The lawyer was a public defender and was supposed to do free work for minors who didn't have any money to get fancy lawyers. "Rosie, you need to remember that they aren't here to be your friend. They will do what they can to try and win the case, but its free legal aide. They don't care. Rosie, a lot of the lawyers are fresh out of law school, so they have to work for legal aid until they get real jobs, or they get noticed by a big time firm that wants to hire them on. So just keep that in your head as well Rosie."

I knew she was right but I kept thinking to myself that it was a lot to remember. There was so much anger in me still I wanted to yell and scream and hit things. Not Chy of course. She kept me calm, I had no idea why. Now that I look back on it I wished I had looked for her more when I got out instead of giving up when I was 18. There was so much pent up rage in me then I wasn't thinking clearly. Hell I'm still not thinking clear on anything in here. Maybe that's why the shock therapy is in play. To shock it either back in me or back out of the darkness that I call my brain. Let me begin about my lovely lawyer. After they brought breakfast in it was shower time.

We got cleaned up and the officer brought us back to the cell. He came back a half hour later and got me and escorted me to a waiting room with two chairs and a table. The room other than that was empty. He told me that the lawyer would be in, in a few moments after they were done checking in and being searched. He added a jab, "Rosie they have to make sure the lawyer isn't smuggling a gun in here for you. We have a little shooter here. We can't have what happened at your house happen here now can we?" I tried to think of a song I liked to tune him out but it didn't work out to well.

I sat there silently and stewed for ten more minutes until the lawyer came in. "Rose? Good morning." She was a small woman about my mom's size neatly dressed in a dark blue suit, pressed white shirt, and short kitten heels, she had on a skirt suit. Why, I'm not sure, but she indeed had a skirt suit on. Why the hell would anyone come to a jail with a bunch of pig cops in a skirt?

"I'll make this brief Rose, my name is Ms. Winters I'll be your legal representation." She sat down across from me and got out two pens and two pads of paper. "Rose here is what I need from you. First and foremost I need you to start by telling me that you will tell me the whole truth and nothing but the truth. If you can do this we can work together. "I thought to myself that she seemed very bold. I replied that it wouldn't be a problem.

"Rose you're being held for shooting your father. Why did you shoot him Rose?"

"Because he was beating my mother ma'am" I replied.

She stopped what she was doing and looked at me. "He was beating her Rose? There's no prior record of that. No records of her being victimized by your dad. Do you realize how this looks?"

"Yes ma'am."

"Rose if he was beating her like you said why didn't you both report it?"

"He threatened to come back and kill us both. He said he would make me pay for all of it. I was the reason she was getting beaten he told me. Ma'am he told me that if he were to go to jail for any of it when he was out he was going to come back and hurt us both. Ma'am he told me that no one would believe me. They wouldn't trust the word of a minor because I was a kid. He said I was no one."

She got quiet and took some notes. When she was done she looked at me. "Rose I realize you and I don't know each other from a fly on the wall, but, you need to realize you are someone. At this time you might be someone who is in a lot of trouble, but Rose you are someone. Don't let anyone ever tell you anything different. From everything you have told me Rose, I don't know if we can get you out of being in trouble completely. But, she continued, I am going to try. You did tell me that your mom never reported the abuse your dad gave her and she lived with that, so that's a hit right there. They will take that into account big time while you're on the stand. You need to remember that. Now there are notes in here about the car ride to the station and you threatening the cops in the squad car Rose. That's going to count against you as well. This trial isn't going to be easy. The cops noted you saying something about if something happened to your mother they were going to be the ones that paid for it. Rose, you said here on the legal pad that I gave you, that they didn't have your mom checked out when the cops got there that night, but there's paperwork in here that states otherwise and a doctor who signed off on it dated the night you were arrested. That's another thing that's going to count against you. I don't know how or why Rose, but this isn't right."

Ms. Winter's continued, "You told me that you weren't read your Miranda rights either. You need to know something... that's illegal. The cops who brought you in should have read them to you; the officer might even swear on the stand that he read them to you, but, with everything that you have told me Rose, the officers in that car will be in a lot of trouble. I don't think I can get you off of all the charges Rose. So there's a good chance that you're going to spend some time in jail. Rose, you need to know as well that they're more than likely going to try and charge you as an adult because you fired a gun with the intent to harm another. Everything we say to each other is clearly confidential. I took an oath. When you go back to your cell tonight if you choose to talk to your cell mate that's up to you. But please heed my warning that she can repeat things to the officers. They can report this to the opposition's legal counsel. Yes that means your dad. I don't know if your father's hired anyone for legal counsel yet, Rose, but if he has the money to burn like it sounds like he does. He could be the type to find someone to burn you on the stand."

"What I'm hoping to see happen, Rose, is that I can get your sentence lowered whatever it might be that they issue to you, I want to see it as low as possible. Like I've told you a few times already I don't think I can get you off of all of the charges completely, but, like I promised you when we began our chat today I'm going to try my damndest."

I looked at her again and said, "Ma'am I'm putting my life in your hands here. I have to trust you."

"No Rose, you don't have to. You're choosing to."

For a moment I almost felt like crying. Other than my mom this was the first person to show me kindness in a long time. Well my lawyer and my cell mate also. I thought for a moment about my cell mate. Was she going to try and hurt me? Would she have used anything we have talked about in the last few days against me to have her own sentence lowered? I wondered about my mother as well, would I see her when the trial began? I tended to wonder why she hadn't been to the jail to visit me. Did he lay his hands on her? Was she bruised and beaten and left for dead? Whatever was meant to happen over the next few days I knew I had to keep strong.

The lawyer had finished up her notes while I muddled through my thoughts. "Rose do you have any questions?"

"No ma'am I don't."

"Rose I'm going to call the guard to come take you back. In the morning I'm going to bring you a change of clothes. You look to be a size eight jeans and a medium size tee shirt. Is that correct?"

"Yes ma'am."

"I'm going to bring you blue, Rose. It's a somber color. I should bring you pink, because it will reflect your age. The fact that you're a young girl might play well for the jury. Pink will be my back up color if I can't find something that works in blue. There will be a clean pair of jeans and underwear as well. I took a look at your clothes that you were brought in with to see originally about getting them cleaned up before the trial, but, they were spattered with blood stains from where you shot your dad. So I cannot very well have you wear that in court now can I?"

"No Ma'am I suppose not."

"What size shoe are you? I'll have to see about some slip on Keds. Really Rose I'm making an attempt here to make you look your age. So the judge and jury will take that into account."

"My shoe size is a 7 ma'am."

"You know I've said this a few times already Rose, but this is a tricky case. Is there anything you haven't told me? Anything at all Rose?"

"No ma'am I don't think so. I think I made sure to tell you everything you needed to know. I mean it's not like you asked me when I got my first period. Which I was eleven if you needed to know. You know I'm a virgin and that the cops harassed me. You also see my grades. Ma'am my grades aren't perfect I'm a middle B student whose home life really fucking sucks. That's about it."

"Rose a lot of that is going to play out to your benefit. I'm going to call the guard now. Please remember what I said about talking to your cell mate. I'll see you in the morning Rose, bright and early. Remember to shower and get squeaky clean so when you get to the court house we can change you. I'll bring the clothes with me like I said." She got up and knocked on the door. The guard came in to walk me back. She left as well. She said not to talk so when she wasn't in the hall with us anymore I thought of my favorite song to tune him out. Officer Jackson. I really wanted to call him officer jackass, but I kept my mouth shut. He brought me down two flights of stairs to my cell, and unlocked the door.

"Nighty night shooter girl" he said and shoved me in.

After the Lawyer

That night Chy looked at me when I came back from meeting with Ms. Winters. "Rosie you were in there for a very long time. Did my advice work did you remain calm?"

"Yes Chy, it worked." I felt like I really needed to heed my lawyer's warning and not talk. I changed the subject. "I'm screwed as it is Chy. So why don't you finish telling me your story. I started to think to myself that it would be easier to keep her distracted until morning. It was 630 at night I pointed out to her 'last call'. She laughed. Here we were two wayward kids in a lot of trouble with the law.

She went to the bathroom. I turned my head so she could have some privacy. I think she liked how I treated her like a sister. I didn't have any real sisters so I guess this was the closest I was going to get. Why not make do with what I had at the moment right? At least there wasn't the rancid smell of urine in here anymore. I think while the lawyer had me busy she must have asked the guard to let her wash her uniform she was wearing. Maybe not, maybe they gave her a clean set of clothes. It made me wonder what she did to get them to be nice to her like that. Never mind Rose I started to think to myself. Put those thoughts out of your head. She's just a nice girl in here who isn't going to hurt you while you're here. Just distract her tonight so you can get through this. You can tell your paranoid lawyer she rubbed off on you in the am. Maybe she would have some respect for me for keeping my mouth shut as instructed. Who the hell knows but I'm going to try it.

"Chy, so you were telling me your story last night about your foster parents. Why were they threatening you? You could have turned them in."

"I could have, Rose, but look where I am now."

"No Chy, that's bullshit. They weren't doing what they were supposed to take care of you guys. You did what you had to to make sure the little kids were eating. I mean yea it was junk food but you did the best you could." She smiled a bit. It looked like a forced smile. "How did they catch you?"

"When I didn't bring home what they asked he started to threaten me again. He told me I needed to go back out. Mind you, it was nine o'clock at night. I needed to bring him home a bottle and a steak. We argued about it for fifteen minutes. It was too late for me to get there before the store closed. I wouldn't have a way to get in there and make sure I really got what he wanted without getting caught. He finally told me to go. He was going to call the cops if I didn't go and say I hit one of the little kids. I went. I walked half way across town. The store was fifteen minutes from closing by the time I got there. I thought if I was careful I could at least grab a bottle from there. There was a cop car parked outside already." She told me she was leery about even walking in. she told me that he never told her what time she had to be back with it. She had fed the little kids a peanut butter sandwich each before she left so she wasn't worried about them not eating. She told me she was going to take her time and not rush back. Maybe if she came back around midnight he would be asleep. Though he was crazy enough to wake up one of the little kids, hurt them, call the cops and say she did it.

She told me she felt like she was screwed and panicked. She told me that she went to walk around some more. She was seventeen so she wouldn't be bothered so much being out past curfew. A few drunks on the corner howled at her. She walked by as fast as she could. They made some cat calls at her. She told me she said nothing and picked her pace up even more. They probably knew her foster dad. As it was all the male drunks in that town ran together it seemed. She told me she walked more towards the other side of town where she knew there was a mom and pop shop that was open late. They sold bottles there. She got one and ran. The cashier was high as a kite. He wasn't paying attention. She brought that back home. By that time it was 12 am. When she got home she was shocked to see him still awake. She handed him the bottle and told him it was all she could get without getting caught. She told him she had to go really far for it too.

"That's not good enough Cheyenne. She told me she started crying. Get the hell out of my sight you little bitch he yelled at her." He cracked open the bottle and took a swig. Chy said she went to the other room and took her shoes off. She went to lay down. She didn't know that her foster dad, fueled with alcohol rage, would call the cops on her. He snuck into her room to see if she was sleeping. She said she must have just dozed off. He woke up the youngest. He smacked her around a bit while he was waiting for the cops to come. He had waited until the red marks weren't the size of his hands to call...the sneaky fuck. He snuck back into her room once more while she was asleep and put the bottle in her room with the cap off. It was by her bed on the floor. The loud sirens were what woke her up. She jumped out of bed. Knocking over the bottle she screamed when it splashed her. What the fuck did he do to her? Her pants were still on and zipper intact. She checked her bra to make sure it wasn't messed with. She raced down the hall to see the kids were with the cops and the youngest had red splotches all over her.

"What the hell was going on, baby girl, are you ok? She ran to her foster sister. What's wrong?" She just cried more. She hid her face. The baby foster sister was told not to look at Chy. If she did she would have told the truth. She would have ratted out the foster parents for setting her up. The truth did end up coming out. The youngest knew she couldn't lie and Chy was locked up for the theft charges but only after the child abuse charges were dropped and scrubbed from her record. She was legally an adult they brought her to jail. They tried to get her on the underage drinking charges but her lawyer fought that. She said that her lawyer even though it was legal aid actually got her off that charge as long as she was willing to plead guilty to all the theft charges. Her foster dad couldn't fake the blood test when her blood was tested for alcohol. He did try to make a mess when she took a breath test. She made the cop listen to her when they pulled her outside. Her baby sister and the other foster kids were all woken up and put in a room with a social worker. The baby sister fessed up and told the truth when the other kids all said that Chy was the best sister they could have hoped for. By the time she was done with that part of her story it was 10:30 pm. I told her we should head to bed.

"You're right Rosie we should. I should get up and go to the restroom first." She went quickly and laid back down.

"Chy it seems like there's more to the story about your foster dad than you're telling me. What else did he do to you? What else made you fear him the way you did?"

"It's nothing Rosie. Let's just go to sleep. He's not going to hurt me anymore."

"He put his hands on you like my dad did to my mom?"

"No Rosie he didn't hit me like he hit your mom. He raped me for two years. It's why I started to eat more and not take care of myself. That way he would leave me alone."

"That's terrible Chy, why didn't you report it?"

"Because Rosie he told me he would kill me. He said that he would slice my throat open while I was sleeping. He told me he would find my little sister and hurt her as well. He told me as well no one would believe a foster kid. I was in there for a reason. A ward of the state. A troubled child. So who would believe me?"

While Cheyenne was telling me this I wanted to throw up. Who the hell would rape a child?

She started again by telling me that her foster dad, when the whole thing started between them, said that his wife was neglecting him and he needed help. He needed to feel loved. He said that she needed to help him. He was always drunk when he came into her room. He said that his wife was too strung out. That was all he worried about. She loved the drugs and not him. He cried in front of her. She gave him a hug, told him she loved him, and called him dad. He kissed her on the mouth. She told me she pushed him away. She told him it wasn't right. She was a child. I'm your child. You aren't supposed to do this. That was when he forced himself on her. He covered her mouth with his hand and told her not to scream or he would hurt her. When he was done he threw a towel at her and said clean yourself up. He blew a kiss at her and walked out the door. At the time she was the only girl in the house so she had the room to herself. There wasn't anyone to see it.

My eyes went wide. I couldn't fathom how someone would do such an insane horrible thing to a teenager. She got very quiet for about twenty minutes. I almost thought she had fallen asleep. She started to talk again. "Rosie I don't want you to feel sorry for me this is my cross to bear. He did this to me. I should have screamed out for help. I should have told my foster mother. I don't know what she would have done about it since she was snorting all that powder up her nose."

"That's just not right Chy. Those people took an oath to care for you and to care for your foster siblings. They should be thrown in jail."

"Oh Rosie, my foster dad did go to jail. I heard from one of the other guards he was beaten the first night he got there. He'll get what he has coming to him. I know stealing is wrong and I'll pay my dues but that man has a special place in hell reserved for him. I'm glad you let me talk it out Rosie. Of course I mean we're stuck with each other. Why not make the best of it? Or worst? I guess it all depends on how you look at it." She just looked at me funny, "You know Rosie you sure have focused on talking about me tonight. Why?"

"That's easy Chy, the lawyer let me talk it out today. So I was repaying her kindness."

"Are you sure Rosie?"

"Yes Chy. Maybe we just need to go to sleep." I guess I wasn't a pro at keeping the subject changed. Maybe she knew I was lying. It got quiet. About thirty minutes later she was snoring. I was left to lay there with my thoughts. Tomorrow was going to break me. I had sworn I wasn't going to let it. As much as it was going to kill me to see him get away with everything he had already done. The worst was over. Now I just needed to pay my price for reacting to him in the worst way I could have. He deserved worse, the piece of shit. Maybe later he would get it. From someone else's hand other than my own.

The lawyer was right. I was in enough trouble as it was. I'm only 17. What you don't realize is that its 12 am and it's my birthday. What a perfect way to spend my day. I should be with my mother having coffee and a slice of pie like we do every year, but I'm here in this cell caged like an animal waiting for my sentence. This sucks. I laid there thinking about it. I wished I hadn't shot him, but it wouldn't have changed anything. It wouldn't have changed how we lived. I knew that much. He would have eventually killed her. He would have killed me as well. When I got out of this mess would I be able to get my job back? I started to mentally beat myself up. I started to cry, tears streamed down my face as I laid there. I covered my mouth with my hand to stifle anything that might betray me and the fact that I was still awake to her. I didn't want to have her wake back up. That was the last thing I wanted, to have to explain. I made Chy do all the talking tonight to hide everything that went on with Ms. Winters today.

  She had a point she didn't know if Chy was a narc. It could all be a figment of her imagination as well as my own, but she was right I couldn't take any chances. I'd rather be later and deal with the mental guilt when all was said and done. I had to wonder if my mom would be there tomorrow. Would she tell the truth if she didn't I would be fucked. I hoped like hell Ms. Winters wouldn't crumble in her cross examination. Even though my mother worked for a lawyer I hoped she had not learned a trick or two from them about cross examination and lying. I hoped and prayed she wouldn't but she needed to save her own skin she might. It was sad that I ever had to think that way, especially of my own mother. The woman who gave me life. It was sad that I had to think of her like that, but I'm in jail at this part of my life and I'm not even eighteen.

  I didn't have thoughts of going to prom. I wasn't very pretty but I shouldn't fucking be here. I should be home studying for finals to maintain my grades. I didn't have plans for going to a fancy college. I would have saved and moved us away. If he didn't have the keys he couldn't get in. If we moved away we could have called the cops if he came in the new house and had him taken away but that didn't happen because I went in commando mode and shot the sorry son of a bitch. I know that I've ranted plenty about him in here, but what parent does that? Where did he get it from? Did my grandparents abuse him? Was he the product of a terrible childhood? Should I feel bad for him? My grandparents were normal people, or as normal as they could be before they passed away. So where did he get it from, or was he just born wrong? Something was just messed up in his head. Did the alcohol trigger it? I mean what was the need to drink like that? Stumbling home at all hours of the night like he did. Did she not want to have sex with him when he came home like that? Is that why he beat her? I even imagine sex with a drunk man... it seems like it would be worthless. My mother would have been lowering her standards even more than she already had by staying with him. The first time he hit her she should have packed us up and left. I should not be here. I should not have had to learn how to shoot a fucking gun by the time I was sixteen. She should have been stronger. Why the hell wasn't she stronger? She was my mother why didn't she protect us? In the last hour that I've been laying here she's snoring and rather loudly which I think is what's keeping me awake. That and all the thoughts I had running through my head about tomorrow. I should make myself sleep. But I am not tired. I should be, I was falling asleep while Chy was telling me her story. Up until she told me about her foster father, his lack of remorse, and the fact he took something sacred to her. Something sacred to every girl. Something she should choose whom it's given to. He could have protected her like he took an oath to. The sorry sack of shit terrorized her and made sure she was thrown in here. I rolled over and looked at the clock on the wall outside of the cell. It was one am. How do I turn my brain off for hours? What would make me sleep? Counting sheep? Probably not. What would happen to my frame of mind? My grades? I would not be able to walk in graduation. Would they let me get my GED in here? I wanted to get up and pace but it would wake her up. Then there would be more questions. More than I was prepared to answer. If I was at home I would have taken a book out to read. I would have been asleep in a half hour. There were no books here. I probably could have asked Ms. Winters for one, but she was new to me. I didn't feel like it was in my best interests to ask a random new person for a book to read myself to sleep. She might have looked at me funny. Maybe she would have said yes. I don't know but I wasn't going to take a chance. I didn't want to push any more than I already had with my case. She probably wasn't going to sleep tonight. She was going to be up all night while she prepared her case. Lord I hope she had some strong arguments. I hoped she was going to be able to trip my father up in his lies. I really hoped that the cops that took me in here would be found guilty of harassing a minor. There were no women present when they brought me in. None. Couldn't that be something bad as well? What if they had tried something funny with me? They were pigs. Who in their right mind harasses a teenager and calls them a slut. Who makes references that a teenager that they had no idea about was a total slut. I mean it was one thing if he was pissed off and mad about his own child, but don't take it out on me. I'm not his child. Everyone in school knew about his daughter. There was even a rumor that she slept with the entire football team. I mean she was a skank, when we were freshman she was suspended for being on the wall ball court with her legs up in the air wrapped around the school's quarter back. She was the slut not me. I had every intention of walking until I was far the fuck away from that insane house to really find who I was and what I wanted. The rumor that was around school, and mind you, it even got to my quiet outcast circle was that she had slept with some biker over the summer who had given her an STD. Like her vagina, she passed those around school as well. So I would never be like her. It would be asking for a Hail Mary, but maybe Ms. Winters would get me down to two years with any luck. I feel like the weight of the world is on my shoulders. My eyes were getting tired as Chy below me let out a loud snore. After that, she started to talk she said no, no, no, not again. I jumped up and woke her up.

"Chy go to the bathroom and wash your face."

"Why Rosie?" She looked dazed and confused.

"You were having a bad dream. So get up and go to the bathroom and wash your face."

"Ok Rosie." I turned my head. I felt bad now. Maybe she was having bad dreams because of me. I made her finish telling her story. I made her relive how that made her feel which I'm sure did a number on her. I wonder if me laying down on the top bunk didn't help much either. Maybe she was feeling all of my thoughts. She laid back down. When she was covered up she quietly whispered, "thank you Rosie. That would have been embarrassing if something had happened again tonight. I really want to get over this problem of mine."

"It's no problem Chy. I just hope they don't separate us after tomorrow or I won't be able to help you anymore."

"I know Rosie, but it will be ok. I'm going to fix this problem somehow." I heard footsteps coming down the hall. Someone was coming to check on us to make sure we weren't causing problems. We both got quiet. I closed my eyes. I guess Chy didn't because when the guard got there she told him that she had to go to the bathroom and she was making sure she didn't wake me up in the process. He must have been new because he didn't even give her a hard time. He just turned to go back to the duty station.

She didn't say another word after that. It was two thirty in the morning by the time I opened my eyes back up. I closed them and lay there again. About thirty minutes later I was out cold.

Trial Morning

When I woke up in the morning it wasn't on my own. The guard came into the cell at 06:00 and spoke really loudly. I jumped out of my sleep and looked at him. "It's time isn't it?" I said. He just nodded.

"You need to shower and eat fast. The bus will be here in one hour to take you to the court house. I guess the cook likes you this morning. He gave you extra eggs and fruit. Eat up I'll be back in fifteen minutes to walk you down to the showers. I just looked at the food I wasn't totally hungry, but I ate. The eggs were rubbery and the fruit wasn't totally fresh, but the effort on the cook's part was there. It filled me up as well. Maybe my lawyer asked that I have a good meal so I would sit and not be jittery during the trial. Perhaps, but that would be one thing I would never come to find out. One of many things to be exact but while I sit here and write this out that is beside the point. I finished up my food and relaxed for five minutes before he came back. When he came back he asked if I was ready. I got up and looked at him. He walked me down stairs and through a badge only entrance and to the showers. I had fifteen minutes to shower and get really cleaned up. I used my time wisely even though the soap bars were dismal. If I got out of the shower to ask for more, the guard would see me naked. I didn't want that. Boy, it was a change from then to a few years ago. I got cleaned up and dressed into a new jail uniform. I went outside two minutes early. The guard looked at me and said I was fast. I just shrugged. He told me that there was thirty minutes to get me upstairs and processed to get on the bus that would take me to the court house. I looked at him and told him that was fine. I knew this

75

was going to be a long day. I didn't get to say good bye to Chy this morning. Why that was I have no idea. I guess they needed to make sure that my head was in the game. No outside help for my mood, though I don't know how she would have helped make it worse. She's kept me calm the last few days. Maybe for her it was all an act. I kept her busy last night telling me about herself. I had to wonder if it was real. She didn't even cry about it. I mean if I had been raped I would at least have been crying when I told someone about it. It struck me as weird. Maybe she processed things differently than I did. Maybe she was hiding something. I wouldn't know because I was being moved after this trial today. I didn't know they had built up enough evidence to make the trial one day, but I was going to find out. We got upstairs to the doors and he checked my ankle shackles as well as my wrist shackles to make sure that they were secure. He quietly whispered that he would be grateful if no one took notice that he was kind to me with the larger portion of food and not being rude to me. He whispered again that he didn't want any problems from the other officers. I smiled and said nothing. He whispered once more that he knew my mom and this was his way of repaying her kindness to him when they were kids. I smiled again. I said nothing as to not betray him. After he was done making sure that the shackles were secured he walked up to the desk and said I was ready for transport.

   "Ready Rose? I'll walk out to the bus with you." I didn't understand why he felt the need to be so nice but I would take it. "Thank you," he said, when we were outside and not in the ear shot of anyone else. "Your mom made my school years easier. I know what happened with your dad. I'm not saying that you did the right thing, but you are a good daughter for trying to protect her. I'll be praying that the jury and the judge see that. Good luck today." I just smiled again not to betray him. "Time to board the bus, kid." He opened the door and said my name to the driver. I was allowed to board after that. There were two guards on the bus already. One was in the front and one in the back. I sat down in the second row from the front, made no sounds, and looked out the window. My shackles didn't allow for much room or moving around so I made myself as comfortable as possible. The bus driver said it was a twenty minute ride. The guard said it was time to go. I was the only prisoner on the bus.

After we pulled out of the gated parking lot the front guard spoke. "When we arrive you should be warned that there might be a lot of angry dock workers there to rally and support your father. There might be a lot of church going women there as well. You need to realize that your father painted you as a harlot to the public eye. Other than telling a lot of my coworkers to fuck off more or less, I don't find you to be a harlot. Mind you, Rose, no one on this bus right now will say what you did was right, but we do understand why you did it. Whereas we don't agree with what our coworkers did to you on your car ride in to the station we hope that your lawyer finds and destroys their credibility on the stand. I had to raise my head to look at them. I mean they lied in your case files young lady. You know it and I know it. Now I'm sorry that it happened to you, and please, Rose, realize as a man and a dad myself, I'm taken aback that you shot him to defend your mom. There were other ways to handle it. Why didn't you ask for help?

I looked him square in the eyes. "Because he told me he would kill us. I know what I did was wrong. I can't take that back, however I can tell the truth. If you're for real like you seem to be, you will indeed pray that the truth is told. There seems to be quite a few corrupt cops. Including ones that like to harass minor girls and call them whores. Calling me a whore when I'm a virgin. The same cop whose daughter is in my school and has slept with the football team. So I don't know who to trust. I want to trust and believe what you're saying right now, but so many people have treated me poorly in my life, even here in the jail over the last few days that I don't know what to believe. It's not easy to say all that, and believe me I really hear what you are saying. I can hear the kindness in your voice, but forgive me if I tell you I have a hard time being kind in return." They got quiet. The driver told us that the bus was five minutes out. He radioed in to the court house. I heard over the CB that the guards were both going to have to walk me in because as they predicted it was a nut house outside. There were dock workers, church marms, high school students, and the virgins club. Yes I really went there the virgins club was there. At one point in time during my high school career I was part of that club before shit got too crazy at my house with the idiot. They thought I dropped out because I decided I wanted to lose my virginity. I just needed to be away from them so they didn't come to my house and witness what he was doing. I heard more come though over the CB. There were signs pickets and a lot of yelling, like I was a pariah. I guess I was to them, because no other teenager had done so, at least not in this town.

The guard spoke again. "Ok kid, when we get there its business as usual. We won't be talking much. There will be one of us on each side of you while we walk you inside." I looked at them. They were pretty big guys. I thought I would be alright. There was only one way to find out. The bus was a half a block away from the court house by then. I looked out the bus window. There were cars lined up back to back. You could hear people chanting. The windows where closed but you could hear sound through them. There were loud chants. My eyes got wide. I looked at the guard.

"Are you sure I'm going to make it in there?"

"Yea kid you're gonna make it in there alright. You know there was always another way. Unfortunately you have to pay the price for shooting him. Part of that is dealing with the devils outside right now. The devils in the dock workers and the little old church ladies who will tell anyone that you're full of sin for pulling that trigger kid...Right down to the virgins club girls who will say you left that club because you were having sex. You need to know that there are people who believe that you're a virgin and I think your lawyer is one of them. You didn't act like a trash ball in jail with any one of the guards to get extra favors. You told them all to fuck off, which for being seventeen years old that's pretty damn brave. You're going to be fine kid. Keep your head down when you walk in between the two of us. Don't respond to anything they say to you.

Don't talk to them either, no matter what. Even if they call you a whore. The dock workers are all your dads' friends. If they scream anything at you don't look at them and don't respond. They are only there to get you more riled up or put fear in you. Remember that." The driver was getting ready to park the bus. The guards both got up and started to get ready to de-board the bus. The guard who was in the back waited while I stood before he got closer. He repeated what the other guard said head down and stay between us. The driver had parked; he started to announce over the loud speaker that everyone out in the crowd needed to back away from the bus. Anyone who didn't would be arrested and held in jail for violating that order. Some of the dock workers didn't back up like they were ordered to. The driver repeated that people need to back away from the bus if or be taken into custody and held on the charges of being a public endangerment. I heard a dock worker yell that I was a public endangerment. I needed to be taught a lesson. The driver radioed in to the officers that were outside to start picking up the dock workers that were not complying with the directive given.

The driver looked back. "Get her ready."

"Ok kid, wrists out and please don't make this hard. We need to put your hands behind your back and recuff them. Again we're going to walk you inside and meet your lawyer and a female guard. They will take you from there. Are you ready ?"

"Yes sir. Alright. Let's go." They fixed my cuffs and we de boarded the bus. One guard in front of me and one guard behind me, and proceeded forward through the crowd. Mind you, I am small so I hid well between the two of them. I did as instructed and kept my head down. The people there left me feeling worse than I already did.

"Whore! Slut! Killer! They shouted. "Is this why you left our club Rose?" They screamed these things over and over like it was just ok. There was a chant of "Send her away, lock her up, we don't want that kind in our town." One person was brave and reached out and shoved me. The guard behind me used his radio that was attached to his uniform to send a message that they needed help in keeping the masses back. I wanted to scream out that they needed to leave me alone but I couldn't. It was only a few more steps to make it to the steps up to the court house door.

The guard behind me in a low voice said, "Just keep going Rose we're almost there." Another hand reached out and shoved me from the side, this time it was harder. I almost fell to my side. The guard in a loud voice said, "Back up" as he caught me before I fell over. I mumbled a low thank you. Over the crowd, I don't think he heard me but I still said it anyway. She taught me manners in addition to teaching me how to shoot that gun. There were cops that started to surround that area where we were walking carrying riot shields. They were using them to move and make the crowd back up. The guard behind me mumbled that it was about fucking time. They should have been set up with these to begin with. Once the crowds were backed up some the chanting didn't stop, but the shoving did, and the being scared that I was going to be pushed over went down as well. There was a door I could see it. We had gotten to the steps and made it up them. What was ten minutes to get through that crowd felt like a lifetime. Why those men and women were so hell bent on verbally and physically assaulting me when my crime had nothing to do with them I didn't know. When my lawyer called me to the stand I would be sure to let them know all about it.

We got inside and through all the check points. My lawyer was there waiting for me with a female guard and a cloth bag. They traded looks and he handed the female guard a set of keys. Ms. Winters spoke quickly and quietly. She said we had one hour to clean up my appearance. The guard rolled her eyes behind Ms. Winters head. She said that she would be accompanying us to the bathroom to make sure there was no funny business. Ms. Winters looked at her square in the eyes and said she would like to know how there would be funny business since everything she had brought in was checked and there wasn't anything other than changing into something that looked a little more age appropriate.

Ms. Winters looked at the guard and said sweetly, "So please lead the way." The guard walked next to me. She repeated again that I needed to make sure there was no funny business.

I looked at her and said "Ma'am I don't mean to be rude but you're three times my size height and width. How can I make funny business when you would and could crush me?"

"That mouth is going to get you in trouble little girl," the guard snapped.

Ms. Winters said, "Rose you need to mind your manners."

"Yes ma'am." and I shut my mouth.

We reached the bathroom and got inside there were two women in there. The guard made them clear out. "Rose you need your hands and feet unshackled. The guard spoke up you can have your hands first and then your feet. Sorry kid it has to be that way."

"Can we at least make sure that I can button my pants up ma'am?" We can uncuff your hands again after your ankles are re done and you can pull the pants up and button them. Like it or not kid those are the rules. We're already extending them a lot by letting you change because of the hour of your trial we were able to extend you the courtesy of changing here. Your lawyer here wouldn't have made it through the gates of the jail before you would have left on the bus to get here. As a mother myself I understand why she's having you change your clothes so you look your age, but as an appointed officer of the law I have to ask you why you didn't go to the cops when you found out he was hitting her."

"Because I was five and who would have believed a five year old? When I got older he told me he would kill us if I turned him in. He said he would serve his time in jail and then track us down and kill us. He would make me pay for turning him in by tying me up and making me watch while he beat the life out of her. He threatened her with watching men rape me and he said he would take pleasure watching it because I was a burden on him. Not once did he pay bills at the house. My mother worked herself to the bone and for what...broken ribs? No self-confidence? She worked her hands and feet to the bone over the last few years and for fucking what?"

"Rose!" Ms. Winters spoke loudly. "That's enough! Let's get you changed." She had already emptied her bag. There were brand new slacks, a pink polo shirt, and slip on sneakers, so I didn't have to fuss with them when I got re shackled. The guard asked me if I was calmed down. I said yes. She proceeded to undo my wrist shackles. Ms. Winters pulled the pink polo shirt from the pile and handed it over to me. In a small sense of modesty I turned myself around and faced the wall while I changed. Once the shirt was over my shoulders I asked her when I turned around, if there was deodorant. They didn't have it in jail. She smiled and handed me a tiny travel size one she picked up as a last minute thing at the gas station this morning. I popped the cap off and ran it under my arms and made a small sigh of relief. My under arms felt better. They didn't offer it in jail because they were afraid that people would eat it and make themselves sick. Less time in the jail cell and more time in the infirmary would make for the inmates feeling like they were in the cushy life. That was something the guards avoided as much as they could.

This might sound odd to you as adults, but you have no idea how much the deodorant means right now. I smiled a small peaceful smile at them both because my underarms had a nice cool feeling. Maybe even at 17 I had a small touch of OCD in regards to how personal smell could affect someone. It felt amazing to not have a stink and a feel of skin rubbing together under my arms that would create a sweat and smell later. They just laughed. I started to laugh myself but thought that they would think differently if they were in my position and the roles were reversed. A small part of me wished they had a chance to walk in my shoes. Maybe they would have a change of heart and see why I shot him. The guard had a kinder look in her eyes. She shackled my hands back together, but in front of me this time and unshackled my feet. Ms. Winters handed me my slacks. I sat down on the floor and used what I could to wiggle myself out of the prison pants. It wasn't hard. They were slip ons and almost like clown pants because I was so skinny. The pants Ms. Winters handed me were tapered which made it harder. I wiggled my legs through and up to my hips and butt. I went to get up and stopped.

"May I have the shoes please so I can get them on before I get up?" Ms. Winters handed them to me; rather, she placed them in front of me so I could wiggle my feet into the slip ons. They were new and snug. I would have blisters on my feet by the end of the day. I suppose I couldn't complain. I would look presentable, and that was kindness I could not replay. When I stood up and completed shoving my feet into the shoes I was ready. I asked the guard to switch the shackles so I could button my pants as well as brush my hair. She smiled and obliged.

I looked at them both. "These are nicer than anything I had at home. Thank you."

"You're welcome Rose." She looked at me and then looked at her watch. "We have thirty minutes left. Your hair is a mess. I have three sisters. I'm going to brush it, braid it, and we will be done with ten minutes to spare." I just looked at her. I sat down again and let her do her thing. My hair was very long and very thick. When she ran her brush through the still wet hair it hurt because there were knots from not having a proper brush and comb over the last two weeks. It took her ten minutes to work her way through my mop. When she was done she started at the top of my hair and worked her magic with a French braid quickly until it fell down the middle of my back. The guard handed her a rubber band to tie it off so her work would not be wasted. She tied it off and announced that she was done. She packed everything up and looked at the guard. "If you need to cuff her hands now go ahead. "We should head to the court room so we can sit down while we have a chance to get in there. It will avoid major commotion. "She packed everything up in her bag and grabbed it and her brief case. She waited for the guard to finish re cuffing my hands. "Let's go" Ms. Winters commanded. "Rose keep your head down while were outside of here. Even if you see your mother. Show no emotion. Save it for the stand. You do not want to give away all your cards before the dealer asks what you're holding." I just looked at her. She was a small odd woman at times. I've only known the woman for two days but she was an old soul. We left the bathroom with the guard. As instructed I kept my head down and followed her. Ms. Winters lead the front and the guard in the back, with me in the middle. Out of the corner of my eye I saw Myka, the cop's daughter. She had this look on her face like she was experiencing a sick sense of pleasure seeing me like this. I kept walking. We rounded the corner. I saw my mother sitting on a bench. When she saw me coming she jumped up and ran over to me. I put my head up and looked the other way. Ms. Winters spoke up again. "At this time ma'am I'm going to ask that you leave your daughter in peace. We need to go into the courtroom and prepare her. I don't need anything interrupting my client's frame of mind right now."

She opened her eyes wide. "I'm her mother."

"Yes, ma'am you are, I'm her lawyer and she's in the position she's in now for defending you. So ma'am I'll tell you again, please go sit down and let my client go into the courtroom in peace. If you cannot comply with that ma'am I'll ask the guard to radio in for help to subdue you." She looked at Ms. Winters and her mouth dropped. She backed away and went and sat back down. The guard said she was a force to be reckoned with. I had to nod in agreement. She was to be a woman of greatness. I hoped that even with my trial it would gain her some form of recognition. She seemed like she really wanted to fight for me. In the next few hours I would find out just how much that really was. We had one more corner to turn to get to the correct court room. My thoughts strayed back to why my mother was a hallway away. Maybe she was using the time to be away from the idiot. Speaking of him I hoped he would start with Ms. Winters. She seemed to have a fire in her today that was unmeasurable to anything I had seen in a long time. I started to hope when all this was over I would be able to measure the fire she has and make something of myself from the mess that my parents helped create for me.

No, this isn't me shifting the blame as to where my problems came from. Merely telling you the root cause of my trouble and where it started. We were at the door to the court room. The guard made a small comment of this is where she departed. Once she handed me off to the guards inside, Ms. Winters opened the door and we walked inside. The idiot and his lawyer were already there. A new guard came up and handed a set of keys to the guard who had been with me for the last hour.

"You're free to return to your post, Alexander." She looked at me "This is where I say good bye, kid. After hearing part of your story my thoughts are with you. Good luck."

She turned to leave. I said, "Thank you." quietly, though I know she heard me. Ms. Winters reminded me that we were in here and not to say a word. Once the judge came in the trial would be in progress. I needed to mind my tongue and not say anything. It would add to my time in jail and make things messier. Unless I was spoken to I wouldn't say a word. We walked to our seats. The idiot mumbled something. His lawyer told him to be quiet. We sat down and waited. The next few hours were going to be hard.

The Trial

I went to jail. I sat in a cell for my first three weeks looking at the wall. Selfishly, I wish she could have done better. Ms. Winters I mean. I knew she tried her best. She fought like hell in court and pulled out every trick in the book. She made my mother cry because she was intimidated by her. She made my sperm donor cringe and fumble about with his words when she asked him what it felt like to beat a woman. He tried to lie but it came out. She made his lawyer blush when she told the jury that it would be a crime if they found me guilty for more than just shooting him in self-defense. A real man would have never hit his wife. He would have cherished her, worshipped her, and kept her safe. There were a lot of women on the jury and church going ones and single mothers at that. They kept their mouths shut but their eyes betrayed them. You could see what Ms. Winters had said. I had wonder if she stayed up all night writing her speeches that she gave. Her argumentation was perfected with zeal. She tore the cops on the stand new assholes when they lied. They said I was a slut who stayed out all night which was far from the truth. The one cop told her I offered him a blow job if they would let me out of the cop car. Ms. Winters made some jaws drop when she told the cop and the jury not only was I a physical virgin my mouth was as well. That I didn't need to partake in oral copulation despite the rumors that they started. The rumors he had had his daughter start. I know it was her. She was there in the courtroom that day. When I got on the stands I watched her smirk. Like she was enjoying watching this. I thought to myself that she was a sick little bitch. Her time would come. She would end up in a hole in life and get another STD that wasn't curable. She wouldn't be able to go to the clinic and fix the problem again. While I was on the stand I made sure to look at her when Ms. Winters was questioning me about my virginity. I said aloud for the whole court to hear that I would be happy to go to the same clinic that cops daughter who started all of the rumors goes to get checked to see if indeed my hymen was in place. The judge had to bang her gavel to silence the court. She told me I was out of line. I apologized to her and the court. I explained myself.

"You see your honor I wouldn't have said that if I didn't have the words whore, slut and prostitute screamed at me this morning. I feel the need to defend myself."

The judge said that where she could see that it would be overwhelming to be pushed screamed at and treated as such there was still no need for disrespect in her court room. She wouldn't have it again. "No problem ma'am it won't happen again." The jury was still in an uproar about my comments. Myka the class whore just sat there with her mouth open. Perhaps she was astonished that two weeks in jail had grown me a set of proverbial balls. Maybe if she walked in my shoes for a week and watched my idiot beat my mother she would change her ways. She wouldn't want to sleep with every living creature that roamed the earth. The prosecuting attorney Mr. Donovan and the idiot's lawyer looked at me when I was on the stand like I was trash. I was trash because I was A-B student, a paralegal and a dock workers daughter who held her own job. But I shot the idiot so I was trash.

He raised his voice a few times and said, "You hated your father. He wouldn't let you go out at night. That's why you shot him isn't it? He didn't like that your mother gave you everything so he set some ground rules and you shot him."

"Sir, Mr. Donovan, with all due respect I shot him because he came home after another night of drinking and carousing around town again. She didn't want to have sex with him. He was beating her because she didn't want to do what you men would call 'perform her wifely duties' and have sex with him while he was drunk out of his mind. In this day and age isn't it illegal to beat a woman regardless of the title wife girlfriend booty call or elsewise? The cycle repeated itself for a very long time. I didn't want her to suffer anymore at his hand." Mr. Donovan plead with the jury that I was out of my mind. They needed to see that I was a teenage girl wanting to go out at night carouse with my friends. Go to parties. Mr. Donovan made it sound as though I shot him because I didn't get my way like a spoiled teenager. The jury murmured as quietly as possible.

When Mr. Donovan was done Ms. Winters was given permission to reexamine the witness. "Rose would you say you're a drinker?"

"I drink coffee, juice, and water ma'am. Now and again mocha but only when allergy season isn't in full swing."

"Is there anything else you drink?"

"No ma'am."

"No vodka?"

"No."

"No rum?"

"No."

"No tequila?"

"No whiskey?"

"No ma'am I like my brain cells. I don't need anything to make me silly."

"Rose would you say that you have friends in high school?"

"No ma'am."

"Rose would you say that you actually had a friend in school?"

"When I was 5."

"Rose, tell me and the judge and jury why you dissolved the friendship?"

"Because ma'am that's when I first saw him hit her. I didn't think it would be a smart idea for any friends I had to take a chance in finding out my family's dirty little secret like that.

The jury murmured quietly again and the courtroom as well. "Rose so would it be safe to say that his home behavior was erratic?"

"He was drunk a lot."

"Is that why you didn't want to have friends or at least close ones? You make it sound like you didn't want them to see what you lived with."

"Yes ma'am that's correct."

"Rose would you say that you left the club you belonged to at school because you were in fear that your teachers and classmates would stop by the house and see what you lived with? See that you had to lock yourself in your room at night because your own mother was afraid that he might come after you too?"

"Yes." There were a few objections that she was leading me to answer questions. She said that she asked the questions to go over the facts. Sheer simple facts that were true and Mr. Donovan had chosen to ignore. The objection was over ruled and Ms. Winters was allowed to proceed.

She asked one final question, "Rose, if I were to subpoena at least 15 of your classmates and make them bring pictures of the parties. Yes ladies and gentlemen of the jury and this court room our children in this town have parties, and they drink and do drugs and lord have mercy ladies and gentlemen they have sex while they are there. But best of all they take pictures recording all of the people there. So if I were to do this would there be pictures of you there Rose?"

"No ma'am."

"Rose would you submit to a drug test? Blood, hair, and urine right now?"

"Yes."

"Rose please tell the court what those results would be."

"They would be negative ma'am. Those results would be negative. If I had drugs in my system they would still be in there now."

"Yes Rose they would. Ladies and gentlemen, she's right, the drugs would still be in her system. If the court would be so kind to look at Rose's grades... Her two A's are in health and science. I had a chance to conference call with her teachers last night. They all said that she was a bright girl. Very quiet, but very bright. Rose, they said, excelled in science as well as health. She expressed interest in going into the medical field. What young girl would put herself in those panties and ruin a chance of going to medical school as well as ruin her chances of being accepted into programs that would further her education? Because we know that those parties are broken up by the cops quite a bit of the time. As well as there recently was a string of teens that were arrested. Rose was not among those teenagers, mind you, ladies and gentlemen of the jury. Seeing as how you were briefed upon entering this court room Rose had no prior record. They started nodding. They had indeed read my file.

"Ms. Winters is that all you have for your client? Yes I rest my case. Young lady you are dismissed from the stand and you may be seated."

Released From Jail

The day I left jail I walked out in cut offs and a Van Halen t-shirt. There was no one there to meet me. Not that I thought anyone would have been there. My mom had no sisters. Her brother passed when I was 8 years old. They gave me the scuffed up shoes I came in with. Not the slip on Keds that the lawyer had given me. They said she had taken them back. I knew better. They gave them to someone else. Ms. Winters had said they would be in lock up with my things that I had been brought in with. My blood stained shirt was gone. She must have insisted that the Van Halen shirt be put in its place so I would have something clean to wear. Walking through the gates I stood outside the jail where I had lived the last year. I looked at it. I would almost miss this place. I slept more in the last year than I have in the last 13. Or so it felt. The cell mates didn't bother me when they found out what I had done. There were a lot of them that were mothers. They told me that they only wished that their kids would have stepped up for them. I had $100 in my pocket from my job. They had me work in the kitchen. While I was there I learned how to cook. My cell mate told me when I got out I'd make some man happy with all the breakfast foods. She told me I made her gain 15 pounds. Considering she was a recovering coke addict, I told her it was a good thing. She hugged me when I was getting ready to leave and wished me luck. "Thanks I'll need it." I was headed home. My first stop was to my mama's grave. The next was to find the asshole sperm donor.

They said I should keep away from him. I knew I needed to say a few things to him before I just let things go. I knew he killed her. I couldn't prove it. Of course not, but I knew he was guilty as much as I knew my name. I almost called Ms. Winters for a ride when I got out of jail. I was going to see him and I knew she wouldn't approve. She would probably drive in the other direction. I walked down the road some to see where the bus stop was. The guard told me it was a hike. I went on for about 15 more minutes. There it was. Of course there were no signs as to when the next bus would be. I didn't have a watch when they brought me in so when I left I didn't have one to wear either. I just shook my head at myself. A year ago I never really wore watches so why would I start now? It felt like forever waiting at that stop. I really wish I had a bottle of water. I had been smart enough to ask for change for the bus when I left. The guard broke a $20 for me. I had 5 busses to take. It would cost me a total of $3 to get there. I was headed home. There was a mission to complete. They didn't tell me I couldn't go, just recommended how bad of an idea it was. I just wanted answers. She was gone. He wouldn't hit me. I knew how to defend myself. The girls taught me basic self-defense in jail. If he got smart and got himself a gun. I couldn't defend myself against that but if he swung at me I would be alright.

The bus finally got there. I ran up the stairs and paid the fare the driver just smiled and handed me a transfer. I sat in the back of the bus away from everyone else. There were a few people who looked back. Mostly nosey old ladies probably wondering what an 18 year old girl was doing coming on to a bus just a short distance away from the jail. I forced myself to smile and look forward. It was easy I knew where I was headed. Life was going to move on.

Once I took care of a few things I would be able to move on. The idiot and the two cops from the car ride. I thought about the jail guard... the first one. The one who harassed me the two weeks before I went to prison. Not the guard who showed me kindness the day of my trial. The piece of shit that shoved me in my jail cell the day I met Ms. Winters. I was going to find the idiots. They were going to talk and admit that they did terrible things. I was going to have fun with my knife while I dismembered him. The lazy sack of shit was no good. He fed for years on her pain and fear. It was how he survived. The driver announced that we were getting close to my first stop. I would need to change busses. I did wonder if the jackass had been notified that I was being released. He was probably so drunk that he didn't pay attention to the mailings that the jail and courts were required to send out. I had two more stops after this. I got out and waited. The driver had told me it was 5 minutes before the next bus was due to come around. They said that the bus was always on time. Never late. Never early.

When I finally got off the last bus I was two blocks from home. I stopped. There was a cafe. I needed food. I ate last at 6 am when the guard woke me up. I had to eat before they processed me out. It was 2 in the afternoon now and I was hungry. I walked into the cafe while it was slow. The bus boy wasn't anyone I knew. Neither was the waitress. Both were good things. The fewer people who saw me the better.

I couldn't take a chance of someone who really knew me well calling the cops. That was a risk. One I was not willing to take. I asked the wait staff if I could sit or needed to be seated. She handed me a menu and looked at me funny. She told me to pick a spot and sit down. There wasn't anyone sitting in the back of the cafe so I went there. After about 5 more minutes she came over to take my order. Since I had lived on pancakes and eggs in jail I ordered breakfast food but I ordered crepes and fresh fruit with coffee. This was to be delightful. The jail had fruit. It was processed fruit in cups with heavy syrup not juice since it was cheaper to buy in stock by the hundreds. I worked in the kitchen mind you. I saw processed food all day long. Some things would change. I would eat better and cleaner. Processed food made me want to brush my teeth seven times to get the film off of it. They looked at me like used meth or some form of drugs because I brushed my teeth so much. I recalled Lola asking me if I was a friend of Crystal. She called me doe eyes again when I asked her who Crystal was. I asked her if she was a new inmate. She called me loca. Like I was crazy since I didn't know what that meant.it was almost funny when she realized how innocent in some aspects of life I was. Fucking little

94

kid you need to grow up and realize you're in prison. You're with grown ass bitches that would gladly slit your throat while you sleep for a pack of cigarettes. I just looked at her and laughed. She almost hit me for laughing. I looked at her again you were in my shoes once Lola. Yea I was kid. Go brush your teeth doe eyes. We both laughed.

I snapped back to reality. The waitress brought me my breakfast I ordered. I thanked her. She walked away and looked back like it was odd to be thanked. Maybe she looked at me like it was someone she knew. 20 minutes later she brought me fresh coffee. I was done with my food by then. It was nice to wash it down with a fresh cup. She looked at me funny again. I called her on it. "That's twice you looked at me funny. Is everything ok ma'am?"

"Yes, miss I just thought you looked like someone I knew."

"I've been out of town for a very long time. I don't think you would know me."

"Maybe. I, just like you said, look like someone you used to know."

"Probably so miss."

I paid my bill. It was $8.53. I left a $10 and two singles with how dead it was. It would probably be the only tip she got all day. Maybe there was a crowd I didn't know about from earlier in the day. Or maybe it had been dead then as well. I got up with the check stub. Found her and told her the money was on the table and walked out. That was a little too close. If she knew who I was there would be trouble later today. I didn't need the cops on me the first day out. I went two blocks down the road towards the opposite direction. The restaurant and my house. Double backed through the side streets and passed the place. I had to think about it. The food was actually shitty. I wasn't sure why I had tipped her so well. Maybe I just wanted to be forgotten. The cemetery wasn't far from here. I needed to take the back streets. I needed to pay my respects. Even just for 15 minutes. I wasn't going to leave anything on the grave that I had been there. There would be a rectory. Someone should be able to give me directions. I started to think again maybe this wasn't a good idea. It would mean more people who would be able to say that I was in this side of town. No this indeed was a bad idea. I needed to mourn her in my own way. I stopped in my tracks. I need to go to back. I needed my money from the bank.

The Bank

After the bank and feeling like an idiot trampled through what I wanted to be a quiet day, I was not in a too pleasant of a mood. The bank teller looked at me and called the manager when I told her I wanted all of my money. She pulled my name and that was when the whispers started. I looked at her square in the eyes. "Yes I am the same person you're whispering about. No I don't think the whispers should continue do you? Oh and for the record pumpkin. I would like my money now and I would like this account closed so I can be on my way out of town." Her eyes got very wide. She didn't know what to make of my assertive attitude. That was fine. She needed to be off of her guard.

"I'm sorry miss. I need to call a manager."

"That's fine. Call your manager. Call the branch manager for that matter. My voice started to get louder. I really don't care. I want my money and I want to leave this institution. You are embarrassing me and I think you need to stop before I find a reason to call your corporate office and register a complaint." I was close to yelling. The branch manager came over. He took my ID. He asked me to follow him.

"Miss, due to the size of the funds in your account. We are going to have to issue you a certified bank check."

"No you see that's where you are wrong. You're going to issue me cash. I deposited all cash and that is what you will give me back." I gave him a face like I had given Lola in prison when she

97

questioned my virginity. I was close to giving him the same face I had given her when she questioned my sexuality. That was a stupid mistake on her part.

I was in the mood to push buttons. "Sir you know who I am. Your teller embarrassed me." He got quiet. He took a form out from his desk. You need to sign here, here and here.

"This form, Rose, is to close your account. You will no longer bank with FFB after today. One of the tellers is counting your cash as we speak. You're quite lucky that your mother, may she rest in peace, was a signer on this account. It would have been closed if she had not been the day you went to prison. Rose I'm not saying what you did was right. You did pay the price for what was done. However I would appreciate you being kinder to my employees."

"Sir, your employee shouldn't have whispered about me. They should have kept their mouths shut and treated me like everyone else. I have less than two days of freedom left before I have to report to my parole officer. I have to go to the other side of town away from this place and find a place to live. Then, manage to get it set up and de loused so I can find some form of job and attempt some form of normal life for being 18 years old with no high school diploma and freshly released from prison. You know this was my college money. They didn't offer me a GED course in prison. So I need to find some place that will allow that. But maybe I'll test out of that. So somewhere down the line I can take an entrance exam to a community college with my parole officers blessing. Maybe she will also help me pick up the pieces of where my life stopped two years ago. I learned how to cook in prison. Maybe I'll find a restaurant on the other side of town that will allow me to work there since I have a record. But really the money it's going to make sure I have a roof over my head food on the table and maybe a phone so my parole officer can get ahold of me if she chooses. He looked at me like I was crazy. His look softened some.

"You have it all planned out. You're going to make something of yourself aren't you Rose?" I guess he realized I wanted to start over. I thought quietly... Lord I hope he did. I hope he wasn't stupid. I hope he didn't call the jackass. Even if he did I was 18 now. He couldn't take the money from me. That was one of the conditions of the account.

"What time is it?" He pushed his sleeve up to check his watch. He let me know it was 4:45 pm. "How much longer is this going to take?"

"The bank is due to close in 15 minutes. You'll be out of here by then." I turned in my chair to see if there was a clock on the wall. There wasn't. I didn't want to look at his face or the old broads at the counter much longer. He spoke again. He asked me one thing about the shooting. "Do you regret it?"

"Regret what sir?"

"Do you regret that you missed? Maybe she would still be alive."

I straightened up some. "Sir, are you asking me something? I've been in enough trouble this last year. I don't need any more. Unless of course in a few weeks it's what butter is on sale so I can make my 12k stretches as long as I possibly can."

"The only thing I'm telling you young lady, off the record of course is that I wish you hadn't missed. She would still be alive today." I looked at him.

"Mister, I just wish I hadn't been afraid when I was a kid. I wish I had learned the power of my own voice. Maybe she would still be alive today." I smiled at sweetly as I could.

"You're right young lady, fear gets the best of us."

"Indeed it does sir. If I could change anything I think I would have asked my lawyer to check in on her more while I was away. Maybe even that would have helped keep her alive as well." The teller walked up with a green zipper bag with a key sticking out of the lock. "Sir the account request you asked me to process. It's all hundreds with the exception of two hundred in small bills in case she has to travel on public transit." She handed him the bag and left. He unlocked it and counted the money out so I could see that it was all there.

I got up and asked him if I could keep the bag. He gave it to me and I put it in the bag that I was given when I was released from prison earlier today. "Thank you sir I'll be on my way. Thank you for all of your help." I walked out of the bank.

Going Home

I went down the street looked before I crossed then went down two blocks more and was at my house. His car wasn't there. The same planter with the painted moon from my 6th grade class was out on the stoop. He was stupid. But was he stupid enough to change the locks and find the spare keys. I was going to find out. There were no other cars that were out there. It didn't take me but 15 minutes to walk here from the bank. Hopefully the manager didn't follow me. I walked up the step put my hand on the planter to tip it on its side just enough so I could see if there was something under there still.

Bingo. Flat spare. Let's see if it still works. The key was basic; it would work in both the front door and the back. There weren't any cars in the neighbor's driveways so they couldn't see me here. I needed a few things. Clothes, I hope he didn't throw out my things. Leggings. Underwear. One or two bras though I didn't have a lot to fill out a bra so it wouldn't be totally noticeable if I didn't have one on. Hopefully he didn't change the locks. Time to test that theory out. I went to the back door off the street so if there were passersby no one would see that his daughter was entering the house.

The key fit the knob. I turned it and the lock clicked to open. I was in. The back door was close to my room. I turned the corner to look inside. It was a mess. The cops had ripped it up last year. He didn't do anything with it other than put his crap in the room to add to the mess. The sight made me itch. I kept that room cleaner than most hospital rooms. I muttered that he was a fucking pig and a drunk. I had to listen carefully to make sure there was no one here. Not one of his whores. No one. There would be less mess to clean up later. I went into the closet. My school bag was there. My books too. I wasn't shocked that he didn't turn them in. That cost the city more money. Lazy fuck.

I emptied the bag and looked through the drawers. There were three clean pairs of underwear. Plus two tee shirts, a pair of cut offs, and a clean bra. I stuffed them in there and emptied out the bag I took from jail into it as well. There was another clean bra stuffed into the back of the drawer. I put it on, took the money bag out from the backpack, made sure the zipper was secured, popped the key lock into place and removed the key. It was going to hurt me later but I stuck the key in my bra so it would be safe. I had enough to take with me. I took a look into the living room. There was his knife on the coffee table along with two empties from his binge last night. One of them had lipstick. He had one of his whores here in my mother's house. A place that he never paid for. I clenched my fist. I picked his knife up and put it in my back pocket. I walked to what used to be my mother's room. The bed was unkempt and there were ripped open condom wrappers scattered on the floor. I started to feel my temper rise more. This piece of shit was screwing other women in this house. This was her house. I heard a car in the drive way. I should sneak out the back and not confront him. I really need to keep my nose clean at least until I was off parole. No, I wanted to confront him. I was going to stay. I went back into my room. I needed to make sure he was alone. You could hear the lock click and the door creeped open. He was on the phone when he came in. so he wouldn't pay attention to the fact that his knife was gone from the table. He went to the kitchen which was right next to my room. I stood away from the door so he wouldn't see my shadow. He said good bye to whoever he was on the phone with and set it down somewhere. He went to the fridge, I heard it open. That was when I came out of the room.

"Why are you still here you sack of shit? You didn't pay for this house." He was bent over looking for a beer. He stood up and turned around.

"You little bitch." I pulled his knife out of my back pocket and opened it.

"I would watch your mouth old man. Now put the beer down and step away from the counter." I walked in the kitchen more. Closer to him. I kicked the chair out. "Sit down you slob. You disgraced this house and her memory. You want to tell me how she died? Because the report that was in the paper she died from natural causes. Who did you have to bribe to get that taken care of? How many times did you smack her around? Did you make her beg for you to stop you sick fuck?"

He spoke. "Rosie you don't understand. She ..."

"Stop with the excuses you lying fuck. You hit her didn't you?" I got close to him. Kicked the leg that I shot over a year ago. He winced in pain.

"They have me doing office work now thanks to your shooting me."

"Old man tomorrow you're not going to be doing anymore office work. You hit her didn't you? How bad was it? Did she stop breathing?"

"I ... I ... I don't know Rose. I hit her and I was drunk. She must've stopped breathing while she was asleep. When I woke up she was dead."

"I kicked him in the leg again. He yelped in pain. Did that feel good pop? I went behind his chair and grabbed his hair. Look me in the eyes and tell me you regret killing her."

"Rose…"

He closed his eyes. I put the knife by his throat. "Answer the question, pop. Do you regret killing her?"

"No Rose I don't. I thought I was rid of you both. But you're here. Now what are you going to do with me?"

"What do you think I should do with you, you piece of shit?"

"Well you can leave and I'll give you a piece of her life insurance money that I have from her policy and I won't say that you were here. Or you can kill me."

"I don't want your blood money pop. You, however, are going to write a confession. And then pop I'm going to put you out of your misery." There was a pad of paper on the table with one of his whore's phone numbers on there. I let go of his hair and walked towards the table. I grabbed it and the pen that was there. "Don't get up. Don't try anything. I will stab you before you write this confession. When they find you they will find you with that and hopefully the cop who finds you will bury your sick demented body in an unmarked hole for people like you." I handed him the paper and pen. "Now write. Your name the date and what you did to her. When you're done you're going to sign it and then toss it back on the table." He did as he was told.

"Rose, what are you going to do with me?"

"That's simple old man I'm going to slit your throat, cut your tongue out and stab you in the heart. Your throat for all the times you yelled at her with your vocal chords, your tongue for all the words you called her though she was always faithful to you. And finally, your heart because you broke hers when you broke your marriage vows. After that I'm going to leave. And you're going to bleed out. Maybe one of your little whores will find you like that."

#

The cop from the car ride to jail was next on my list. The dirty fuck was removed from the force after my trial because they didn't want a police officer on the force who harassed teenagers, much less women. They started looking into him more and they found him guilty of a lot of things. They had to make sure that their force wasn't being run by corrupt cops. I read in the paper that he caroused with hookers and took bribes as well when I was in jail. It sure did explain a lot about his daughter and how easy she was. I was in a motel for the night. L had some hood rat buy me a bottle and I paid $25 for a room at the 'no tell' motel. I needed a drink. I hadn't before that night. But I killed that fuck and I watched and took pleasure in seeing him bleed out.

Now it was on to the next asshole that terrorized me and reign hell. It wasn't hard to find him. All I had to look for was a huge amount of hookers and I was in business. There was a somewhat very seedy bar in the far corner of town. I went to the nearby bus station and stashed my bags. I would be back for them later that night. I grabbed my hoodie and stuck my gun in the back waist band of my shorts. My knife was in my shorts pocket. When I was at the hotel last night I bleached it clean from the idiot's blood. After I stashed everything I walked to the bar. It was 6 pm and the night life in that side of town was just starting to kick up. It was still early so there wasn't a bouncer outside. I walked in with no problem. Sat down and ordered a plate. They had a dry baked ziti on the menu for the night. It was like chewing cardboard. The bartender brought it out and looked me up and down. I handed him a $20 and asked for a refill on my soda. He just laughed and walked away. He came back five minutes later with a full cup. "You look like someone who shouldn't be in here little girl."

The door was open. "I'm a paying customer. My money's legit. I watched you run it under the black light and run a pen over it when you were at the bar. So unless there's a problem me can I eat my dinner in peace?" He just laughed and walked away. I slowly ate my cardboard dinner and drank my soda and waited. He watched me from the bar. I didn't know it at the time but we would meet again. Finally at seven the cop showed up. I had my hair down which made me look a little different and it had been a little over a year since he had seen me. He went to the bar and sat his fat ass down. I could hear him order a drink. The smart ass bartender told him he should go easy tonight, or he would poison his liver again.

The fat fuck just laughed. "I'm retired and I don't have any regrets. Now pour me a drink you fucking idiot and be generous with the vodka." The bartender shrugged off his comment and poured.

"Are we opening a tab tonight Sarge or are you paying in cash. Open the tab I'll be here awhile. The fuckin' women at my house are driving me insane. So hopefully if I leave here late enough the hens won't be awake and clucking."

"Sarge, that kid of yours have her baby?"

"Yea two weeks ago. The fuckin' brats already whining how hard parenthood is."

"Oh yeah Sarge? Maybe she should take a page out of your playbook and dump her kid off on her baby daddy and go out for a couple hours. I'm sure the boys down town miss her. Or don't you miss having to go pick her up at 12am when she broke curfew."

There was a small stroke of silence. The fat fuck took a drink and told him to go fuck himself. Everyone laughed. A barfly walked up to him and kissed him. He kissed her back and smacked her ass. The display made me sick to my stomach a bit. She looked at least ten to fifteen years younger than him. Her skirt was really short almost to her crotch. She had shiny black open toe high heels on. Her makeup was poorly done. Bright red lipstick and dark eyeshadow. Her hair was poufed out like she used a can of Aqua Net to keep it in place. I knew I wasn't supposed to be in there. So I didn't walk up to the bar when my drink was empty. I waited until he came back over to ask me if I wanted a refill.

I sat and watched the 'Sarge' while he flirted with another woman who wasn't his wife. The T.V. in the bar was just over his head, so it was really easy to pretend like I was watching a sports game. While I was in jail the girls taught me that it was easy to pick a team and who would win. It didn't matter how cute the players were. Just the team and how they paid attention to who was on base. I pretended to amuse myself with that while he did his thing at the bar and got drunker by the minute. He got up and went to the bathroom. I waited until he came back out. I went to the bathroom to check it out. I wanted to see what would happen if I cornered him in there. The bathroom was a small hole in the wall like the bar itself. There was enough space to drop your pants and wipe your ass. There was a small sink outside the bathroom just large enough to wash your hands. This piece of shit hole in the wall bar could at least have a men's and women's bathroom. It would be a bright idea, with the seedy characters in here. It's probably where the hookers took their johns to get them off. Let them test the products before they took them back to the 'no tell' motel that I stayed at last night. I went back out to my table and noticed my plate and cup were gone. I looked at the bartender I raised my pointer finger and wiggled it with a come here.

He smirked and walked over. "You're still here."

"Yeah I am. I'd like another soda please. I sat back down at the table, looked up at him and smiled sweetly.

"Coke, Dr Pepper, Sprite..." I looked at the clock.

"Sprite." I don't want to live on the edge and have a darker soda this late at night." I was really thinking I needed to make sure that they didn't slip anything into my drink. I was here to make him pay for all the lies he told. I was here to cause him pain because he caused my mother more suffering and I wasn't going to stop. The bartender just smirked.

"One sprite coming right up ill missy."

He brought it over. I smiled and handed him a $5, I told him to keep the change. He muttered something about me being a big tipper while he walked away. I sat there while I sipped my soda and watched the Sarge. He had just ordered another drink. He had already knocked back three. I didn't know how high his tolerance was so I would sit and wait.

The lady he was with was joined by another. This one was red headed. She was wearing a tight black halter dress again like her friend the dress was up to her crotch. One false move and all her goods would be exposed. She couldn't walk in heels she toddled. The site was a bit ridiculous. She joined the Sarge and his lady friend. He looked surprised when she came up. Her pal muttered that he need not worry. It would be a night he wouldn't forget. I thought to myself that he sure wouldn't. This was to be his last night on this earth.

A boy came up to me while I was pretending to watch the T.V. "Good game huh?"

I just looked up smiled and said "Yea, its ok I guess."

"Mind if I sit down?"

"Yes actually I do. I came in for dinner and some alone time so I can reflect."

He looked hurt. "Ok then I'll go sit over there. Sorry to have bothered you."

"It's no bother. You didn't know I needed some quiet time in my life." He turned on his heels and walked away. I thought to myself that he was just an idiot looking to pick up a barfly. He was looking to get lucky. He was wrong. I was a virgin when I went to jail and thankfully I was a virgin when I came out. I didn't plan on losing it to some piece of shit like him. I looked down at the soda and took a sip of it. I looked up at the Sarge again. He was flanked on the right and left with the two women. I heard one of them say baby, we should go somewhere private. The three of us. The Sarge looked and said as tempting as it was he wanted to wait a bit more. He needed a few more drinks. It sounded like what one of the girls in jail had told me about. The Sarge needed more alcohol to keep his little Willie up during sex. He needed a little something to keep him up or even excited. I almost let out a laugh when I thought about it. The Sarge was such a big man, he claimed, and treated me like shit. Made sure my father wasn't put away for the violence he caused. He helped allow my mother's death to play out in violence. I didn't know then but I would find out later how close of friends they were. I almost slipped again with another giggle. Such a big man he couldn't keep his dick hard. The Sarge looked around the bar. He scanned the crowd. I looked down and drank my soda looked at my fingernails. I played like I needed a manicure. My nails indeed looked like shit. Spend a year in jail and you tell me how your nails look. It's not like I had salon treatments there. I don't think Sarge wanted his dirty little secret to get out. At least not to people he wasn't paying to keep their mouth shut. Since the papers showed he was excused from the police force. I wondered where he got his money for hookers. Then I remembered. The Sarge was Sergeant Johnson. Mrs. Johnson, his wife, was a trust fund baby. He married money. Lord knows that he couldn't have afforded bar trips on a cops salary with a wife and a kid. His wife's money funded his escapades of drinking and loose women. His wife didn't pay attention to where he scurried off to anymore when the sun started to go down. After his daughter got knocked up and recently gave birth, her attention was needed elsewhere. She didn't need to hen peck on her pig husband. The dirt bag was a real piece of work. He ordered another drink he was starting to laugh at something one of his lady friends said. I drank my soda and waited. The clock on the other side of the bar read that it was 9pm his lady friends finally ordered drinks by then. He was half in the bag. The Sarge fondled both of their breasts. I wanted to barf. He was married for fuck sake. Like the idiot I guessed there were more like him. Why get married if all you were going to do is cheat on your spouse? What was the point of it? I knew I wasn't going to get married. If they found the idiot tonight I was probably going to end up back in jail. After I took care of the Sarge I was getting out of town. I knew that much. I couldn't go after the Sarge's partner from the car ride that night. He was killed in the line of fire after I went to jail.

Hopefully for him he was in one of the lower rings of hell. The piece of shit could have stopped it. He could have told the truth. There was no honorable cop funeral for him. He had been on the take. It came out that he was under investigation. My trial had triggered his IA investigation. The falsified paperwork was only the icing on the cake. There was over 500,000 in cash that wasn't accounted for. 200 pounds of cocaine that went missing from the drug lock up. I had to shake my head while I faked watching TV it was at the right time, one of the teams had lost. The bartender came over with a refill at the same time.

"Hopefully you didn't have any money on that game."

"No I was just rooting for them. They're a strong team. Maybe they just had a bad game." I pulled two dollars out of my pocket to tip him. He told me I was a big spender while he walked away.

"At least I tip. Didn't you just complain that other people left you a dollar? Or even the change from their drink which was what 50 cents? Don't you make most of your money from tips?" He just smirked and kept walking back behind the bar. Douchebag I thought but I didn't say it aloud. I looked up at the clock and it read 9:45. I was weirded out a bit that I had been here three hours and had not been able to make a move. I'd had been out of jail for a little over twenty four hours I didn't have plans on going back any time soon. So I needed to cool my jets. Fifteen minutes later he ordered another drink. He told the girls to kiss each other. They did, it wasn't anything I had not seen in jail. He took a twenty out of his wallet for each of them. He gave them both the money and said that he was almost ready. He was eight or nine drinks in the bag by then. All hard alcohol. He kissed both the girls. We're ready to leave when you are baby the brunette told him. I wanted to puke in my mouth. He got up wobbled a little when he walked to the bathroom. I thought to myself I was going to have to follow them back to whatever shithole they were going to for his good time.

He came back and looked in his jacket for a pack of cigarettes. The lard ass fumbled some looking for a lighter. There were two doors to the bar; the main entrance and then there was a small fire door. He was wobbly while he walked so he went to the back door. He told the red head of the two to come with him. He told the brunette to stay there and watch his jacket while they went out to smoke. As he walked out side with her behind me you could hear him say that she was new so she was going to find out how he did things. That told me she was the new girl to the group. Even though he was a total pig he had a regular mistress. Maybe he worried about STDs for when he finally decided to stick it to his wife. I heard the bartender ask the brunette how business was. She said that she was getting out of the life soon; she was old and needed to be done. She looked like she was thirty but maybe she was older, maybe she wanted to retire. Retire from what?! Being a hooker? What kind of job skills did she have? I mean did her dates even give her enough money to start school? Get an education?

Maybe she did who the hell was I to judge? I wouldn't harm her or her friend I decided. They didn't harm me in my trial. They didn't harm my mother either. Five minutes later the Sarge came back inside licking his fat nasty fingers. I could only guess what had transpired outside. She walked back inside behind him with a smile on her face. A stupid silly little grin. Stupid bitch you gave it up to that fat pig to easy. And for what another twenty or maybe forty? He seemed like a cheap piece of shit. They walked back to the bar. The brunette got up from his chair. She called him baby when he sat back down. We're leaving in twenty minutes girls so make sure you get your drinks. Have some more of the snacks here that Matty boy here put out for us. So that was the bartender's name. Matt. He looked like a real douche. I looked across the bar to see if lonely boy was still there. He was, he was staring right at me. It was like he was trying to catch my eye. I had to wonder what his motives were. Maybe I would come back after I took care of my business with the Sarge. I would see if he was still here. I smirked when I looked him in the eyes. He looked innocent but then again so did the red head. Look what her profession was. I had to wonder what he was and who he was. The two ladies with Sarge had a few drinks. I think the red head had a soda so she would be more aware of what happened to her later. At least that's what Lola told me in jail. She was a hooker. She told me she would have sodas instead of mixed drinks so she was aware of what was going on around her. She got popped for possession and propositioning an undercover cop. The jail stories and rummy. I could fill this journal for a very long time with some of the things those girls told me. They called me doe eyes for the first two months I was in jail. They named me that because I was in shock with some of the things that came out of their mouths. It wasn't like I knew life, or their version of life. I was going to make my own. I for the tenth time since I woke up swore to myself I wasn't going back to jail. I looked back at the bar where Sarge and his ladies were paying their bill. I didn't owe any money but I would leave two more dollars on the table where I had been sitting for the last six hours while I watched them. I thought to myself that the Sarge should have recognized me by now. Maybe he was just an idiot like the other one I no longer shared

DNA with. They got ready to leave, made way to the door. Matty the bartender yelled out, "See you in an hour Sarge."

The Sarge yelled back, "Fuck you Matty." He just laughed and laughed. You could hear Matty mutter that he was a piece of shit and a crappy tipper. I looked up and pretended to check the time. Instead of two dollars I left four. Maybe he would keep his mouth shut when I walked out. I pulled the small bills out of my back pocket. I dropped them on the table.

I walked to the exit past the newly stationed bouncer. "Good night."

I looked at him and smiled. "Yes I think it's going to be." I turned and walked away in the direction I had seen them turn. I had every intention of knocking on their door giving both those girls $100 each so they would leave quickly when I got to the motel. They were getting to the third floor from the stairs, walking down the hallway. It was three doors down from the staircase. They went inside. I started walking up the stairs slowly. I checked my waistband and made sure I was good to go. That piece of shit was going to pay. I made it to the third floor; I went to the third door down. I could hear them both they sounded like they were laughing but faking it. He must be super nasty to look at. I walked back to the stairs; I sat down for five minutes. I waited. The time passed really slowly. I got back up and walked over to the door and knocked. I pulled the gun out of my waist band. I stuck it in my back pocket. I could hear one of them say they would get the door. The brunette answered the door, I pulled my gun out.

"Go back inside, get your shit, get your friend, and get the fuck out of here." I pulled $500 out of my front pocket tossed it at her. That was a lot more than I planned on giving them. That's more than you'd get from this clown in two nights. Share it between the both of you. Whatever the fuck you do you won't repeat what you saw here tonight or I will come back and find you both and skin you alive. Their eyes got wide. They got their shoes back on grabbed their purses and fled. The red head looked scared. She was going home and staying there, she was out of this night life. The brunette called me a crazy bitch when she was running out the door. I turned and looked at the Sarge he was tied up on the bed with a blind fold. This was too easy.

"What the hell is going on here? I can't move... girls?"

"They left. It's just you and me you piece of shit."

"Who the fuck is there?"

"Oh Sarge you probably don't remember me. You lied on the stand last year you put me away. Do you remember now? You signed my mother's death certificate the day you did that. Now do you know who I am?"

"Oh fuck, you're that kid who shot her father. The one who was beating on his old lady. Yea I remember now. You come here of all places. You were watching me at the bar weren't you? You're some kind of stalker aren't you? What have you been out of jail a day? Maybe two? I started to wiggle his hands to get them out of the hand cuffs he was in. I cocked the gun back and he froze. "You're going to shoot me?"

"Yea Sarge I am. But you're going to pull the trigger yourself and do it for me." I handed him the gun and got his handcuff undone. "Put the barrel in your mouth. Pull the trigger, you sorry sack of shit."

"Tell me why you're letting me end my life."

"Because, you piece of shit, you chose not to help my mother."

"He paid me to do what I did. He paid me 2,000 large to lie and harass you like that on the stand."

"That's ok, Sarge, he has been taken care of. Now you're delaying my plans. Pull the fucking trigger you fat sack of crap." He put the barrel in his mouth. Almost as if on command he pulled the trigger. There was a small explosion sound when he pulled it. Two seconds later he was gone. I never took the blind fold off of him. I took two fingers and carefully took off his blind fold. He had watery eyes in all the mess of his brains. I smiled a little bit. He was scared when he died. I breathed a small sigh of relief. My trouble was gone. The fat fuck took his own life and took his punishment like a man. I grabbed my gun put it in my waist band under the sweatshirt turned the stereo down and left the hotel room. I walked down the three flights of stairs and into the night. I almost went back to the bar to check that lonely boy out but I didn't. I headed to the bus depot to pick up my things. I put the gun and knife back in my bag. I pulled some money out of my bag to buy a ticket to leave.

The ticket agent looked at me "You're a little young aren't you, to be traveling this late at night?"

"No sir I'm eighteen and legal. I'm headed out of this dump to begin a new life." He sold me my ticket. I went to the waiting area. There was a ten minute wait. The bus was really empty from the looks of it. There were three other riders besides myself. One driver was out across the street smoking. I boarded the bus and sat down in the front so I could give him my ticket. There was five minutes left until we were due to take off. He stubbed out his cigarette, walked across the street and boarded the bus. I handed him my ticket and he gave me a stub back. I went to the back of the bus to go to sleep.

St. Louis-The Hotel

I got out of the bus terminal in St. Louis. The Greyhound terminal was nearly empty. It was 3 am. I wasn't sure where I should go so I walked around looking at some of the signs. There was a hotel two more blocks down. I had a lot of cash on me so paying wouldn't be an issue. There was a guy on the corner who looked like he was watching me. I wasn't sure so I crossed the street in the middle to avoid him. The hotel was half a block away. I couldn't hear any foot steps behind me which was no skin off my back. I got there in two minutes. I entered the hotel. The desk clerk was heavy set with orangey bronze hair. Super painted on eyebrows. Bright blue eye shadow. She looked like she belonged in the circus or with the actress *Divine*. If you ask me she was scary. When she spoke I had to wonder if she was a man.

"I need a room please."

"For how long?"

"Two weeks... maybe three."

"That's a long time are you new here?"

"Yes, I just got in tonight. I'm super tired. How much is the room? I have cash. I can pay for the whole thing outright. I pulled $1000 out of my front pocket. Her eyes got really wide at the sight of that much cash."

"Do you have some ID?"

I faked like I was checking my pockets. "Oh no I don't. I must have lost it on the bus or in the terminals when I was getting on the bus or getting out."

"Well I don't know if I can book a room for you without an ID."

I pulled out an extra $300. "Look, I'll pay an extra deposit if I have to. I am so tired. I really want to lie down." She just looked at me for 30 seconds. She went to deny me again. I had to give a face like I was going to ask for her manager. Which seemed to make a difference. I spoke again "I'm offering to pay for everything outright and pay more than the deposit. I just told you I traveled way more than the average person in one night." She looked at me again. "Is your manager around?" She just gave me a look like who was I to ask for her manager. Perhaps she had decided that it wouldn't be a good idea for her manager to come down stairs. She quickly changed her attitude.

"There's no need to call him. I'll take your deposit and, the three weeks up front."

I looked at her. "I'd like receipts for all of it please." I gave her a look like don't you dare put my money in your pocket bitch. Maybe I learned a thing or two while I was in prison. The girls there told me I was too nice. They were going to toughen me up some. They didn't beat me to toughen me up. They made sure to teach me to not take any shit. Lola said to me, not from a man not from a woman. She then said not from a grown ass woman with an attitude problem.

The desk clerk gave me another look like I was brazen for making sure all of my money was accounted for. It didn't really matter much. With her attitude problem and sneaky face I was going to make sure I had receipts. I knew there would come a day where I would check out from here and I wanted all my money back. She came with three sheets of paper for me to sign. I signed my mother's first name and then my own first name for my last name.

This would be my new name from now on. Tomorrow I would look for a job at a diner. Tonight I was going to sleep. She commented that my name was pretty. I said thank you. She looked me up and down. Kind of like I was going to cause hell. I knew I wasn't. I picked the room key up and saw she put me on the third floor. At least I only had my backpack. I had spent a lot of money in the last few days. There was no way I was spending any more in that amount any time soon. Two thousand five hundred was gone. At least five hundred of it was from the idiot's wallet. He didn't need it where he was going that night? He got a one way bus ticket to hell and I was his driver.

"Is there an elevator here? Or just stairs?"

She looked at me like I was an idiot. I must have asked her the stupidest question she had heard all day. "There's an elevator. This isn't the 1800's. Go down the hallway make a right and it will be right there. Just follow the signs when you get upstairs and you'll find your room."

"Thank you." I started to walk away. I stopped and turned around, "Is there food service here?"

"There's bagels cream cheese and fruit in the morning. If you want coffee there's a diner two blocks away from here. This isn't a fancy hotel. There aren't coffee makers in the room. There's a vending machine on the bottom floor. The guy comes tomorrow to fill it up. There's a sign on the inside of the door if you need room service for cleaning. There's also a do not disturb sign. You look like you're about 18. This isn't a no tell motel. Don't have a bunch of men running in and out of here all night long. You're a pretty little young thing too. If you're part of a service don't let your pimp make a mess here either. Don't invite him here either. This isn't going to be a place for that either."

I just looked at her. "Maybe you didn't understand me. I just got off the Greyhound bus. That's #1 I'm a virgin that's #2 I'm not looking for a bitch fight that's #3. Maybe you need a smack of reality or maybe I need to wake your manager up and let him know that you're really upsetting paying customers."

"As you say I'm not looking for a bitch fight either. But I do need to make all of our guests aware of the rules. If you can't abide by them you will be asked to leave. And your security deposits will not be refunded."

"Do me a favor." I squinted at her name badge again. It read Annabelle. "Call your manager. I'd like to speak with him." She must have not realized who she was dealing with. But I sure as hell wasn't going to be insulted right when I walked into a place.

"You really don't need to make a scene here" she told me.

"Yes I think I do. Within the last half hour you called me a whore and pretty much insisted that I'm a street walker. So please let's call your manager. You do realize we're being recorded." I looked up and pointed to the video camera. "I'm pretty sure there's sound attached to it as well." She picked up the phone and pressed a few buttons. I guess she was willing to call my bluff.

"Hello Mitch I need you to come down stairs. We have a situation." She raised one of her painted on eyebrows. "Ok I'll see you in a minute. She put the phone down. He's on his way dearie. Why don't you sit down and rest after your long travel." I didn't have time or the want to sit. I was ticked. Almost too where I wanted to get my gun out and shoot her. Annoying bitch. The office door behind her swung open. A skinny little man walked out. He was bald with a badly shaped beard. The mustache was entirely too bushy to match the rest of his face.

"Hello miss I'm the night manager here. My name is Mitch. What seems to be the problem?"

119

"Sir, I just came in from Virginia on the Greyhound. I lost my ID. I paid cash up front for 3 weeks to stay here and two security deposits. Your clerk, Annabelle, in the matter of the last five minutes has implied that I'm a hooker. I work for a service and there needs to not be a lot of men running in and out of my room at all hours of the night. Now maybe it's my cut offs and tee shirt but don't most hookers dress better at least the ones I've seen on the two cops shows do."

He looked at me like I was high as a kite. "You need to calm down" he said.

I pointed to the video camera. "That records doesn't it?"

"Yes it does. I'm sorry I didn't catch your name."

"Its Katherine, Katherine Rose. And mind you I was on a good one. Is there audio as well?"

"Yes there is."

"So if you were to go in the back and listen to the tapes you would hear everything wouldn't you?"

"Yes I would. Miss Rose. What would you like me to do here?"

"Honestly I'd like you to force her to apologize and think about refunding some of my second deposit I made. Or moving it to a 4th week of money on my room. Mind you its 4 am. I'm tired and I'd like to go to sleep soon." He looked at me thoughtfully and nodded in agreement.

"Annabelle, you owe this young lady an apology. This will be going on your permanent employee record. Miss Rose if you will give me a moment to fix the paperwork here." He changed the end date of my stay at the hotel by one week and refunded my second deposit that I made since I lost my ID This was perfect. I had one extra week to get my shit together. Tomorrow I would go find someone who would make me an ID. I would look into the diner and see if they would hire me.

Finding Katherine

The room was far from perfect. There were two clean pillows on the bed. The air conditioner was on. I looked for the switch. There was a little too much sound for me at the moment. In two days' time I had killed two men and ran 400 miles away from where I should be. In a few hours I should be checking into my parole officers' office. I was miles away from there. In the morning I would need a hair color and cut. My hair was down past my ass now. I would take it to my shoulders or shorter. I could pay them to color it at a salon. I'm white blonde mind you. I could really go any color that I wanted. I had no real base color to stop me from being a red head or even raven black. I would do that before I got myself a new ID so it would look legitimate. If they were going to look for someone they would have to try hard. I would need to make sure that the job I found myself was off books. Waitressing for tips would more than likely be the best I would be able to do. This is St Louis. I have a month here. If nothing changed I'd move on and away from here. I would take my new identity with me and start over yet again in a new city.

I sat down on the bed. Should I sleep? Or should I get up and find a salon that I should go to in the am? It's still dark outside. Its only 5 am. Sleep. I needed to stop tomorrow and buy a few things as well. A real bra for starters. Underwear and a skirt or two. Some dress shirts so I looked nice when I went to find a job, and a purse. This backpack wasn't going to find me shit. I looked homeless. Which wasn't good. You could tell it was old. You could feel the springs through the mattress. The pillows were thin as well. It was clean. I was starting to regret what I had paid money on, but I needed to get out of the street. I got up again and made sure the door was locked. I checked that my gun and knife were stowed under the bed. I unlocked the door one more time and opened it. I put the do not disturb sign up just in case I slept until noon. I didn't want some maid walking in and finding my gun while I was sleeping. I wasn't sure about my new best friend down stairs. She looked like the type to cause problems if I let her. The gun was registered in my dead mother's name. Maybe when I woke up I would look for a storage locker for them. That might pose an issue with no ID. I would find one. I needed to deep clean it as well. It stank and the powder on it was black on my hands whenever I touched it. I locked the door one more time and went to lie back down. It was about an hour before I went to sleep. When I woke up it was 11 am. I stretched out and it hurt. I'm 18. I shouldn't feel like this. I can't straighten out my back for my life. Perhaps I could find a massage place today. If I paid $100 for it, it would be worth it. I looked in my bag to see the clothes I had brought with me. I needed something halfway decent. Maybe I wouldn't get kicked out of stores. There was a pair of leggings and an oversized tee shirt. I pulled that out. I hadn't worn the shirt in a long time. I was skinny when I went in jail for the first time. The shirt then was big. The fact that I had gained some weight made it not so tent like but just baggy. Which was good, but, I still had some room to fill out. I didn't have much of an ass either. I headed towards the shower to see how crummy it looked. I needed to see how small the shower was. There was nothing I wanted more than to take a bubble bath and a razor to shave my legs. I did a crap job two nights ago. But you don't shave well after you down a whole bottle of liquor. It's usually not a safe idea either. Regardless, that indeed, is what I was going to do tonight. I looked in the bathroom. It was super cramped. This didn't look appealing at all. There wasn't enough space for me to stretch out in the shower to shave. Oh well that's the price you pay for cheap living. It was a shame to have spent hard earned college money on a hotel to hide out in. I would say I had emotions about killing those two bastards but I don't. I turned my emotions off. And really yes it was my gun that killed him. But the Sarge is the one who pulled the trigger. Maybe I forced his hand on it, but my mother dying and his lies forced mine.I would add bleach to my list of things I needed here. The floor felt gross underneath my feet. I had no idea the last time it had been cleaned but it felt like there was a wax substance underneath my feet. I got in the shower and turned the water on. The small soap bottles that were in here would do for now. My hair was down past my ass I would need a real bottle of shampoo and conditioner if I wanted to maintain this look. I probably wouldn't maintain long hair after today; I was going to cut it off, so I could blend in more. I thought about it as I stood under the water. I need to wash being over tired off of me. About 20 minutes later I got out feeling like it beat me up but better than when I went in.

Maybe I would stop at a tattoo shop today. I didn't have any tattoos even when they wanted me to get one in jail. If I were to get one it would have to be hidden on my ribs. I wanted a dove. It meant something that would hold a lot of weight. I was finally at peace. Maybe my mother would be able to rest in peace. She was probably ashamed of me. Of what I did. I wouldn't be able to take that back now. She would still be here if they had done their jobs. The cop should have told him no. He shouldn't have harassed me. He shouldn't have encouraged his cunt daughter to lie. She got hers in the end. She has a child now. I didn't see her while I was there. I would have told her she had gotten her just desserts. She wouldn't have a life passed feeding her kid and making sure the baby's diaper was changed. It was hard to imagine the class whore doing that, but hey, it happens to the best of them... or rather the worst of them. She was destined to a life of lying on her back and spreading her legs to find a minute or two of love. There wasn't going to be a man who wanted a readymade family. Her mother would probably let her stay at home since she had money, but Myka was stupid. She would push and push and force hands to where her perfect little life would unravel more and more. Her dad wasn't there anymore, but he never really was. That was how she got knocked up to begin with. She had a dad and now she didn't anymore. An eye for an eye. She helped take my mother away. Her father was the price she had to pay. The baby she had was far too young for its mother to be taken from him. When it came to that family I was heartless, but I wasn't that heartless. Just because his mother was a liar and a whore… he wasn't. So I wouldn't harm his future. Hopefully, he would learn what she was when he was older. He would then be able to decide whether or not he wanted to deal with her. Would I go back and tell him his mother's sins. No. She would all on her own.

I got dressed and ready to go. When I walked down stairs Annabelle was there. She looked at me funny. Maybe it was because I was all covered up. I didn't have my cut offs like I did 5 hours ago. My shirt was very long and baggy. I smiled at her and waved on my way out the door. She just looked at me like I was crazy. I had all my cash with me. I had my gun too. I was going to find a home for it. Clean it, and store it away where no one had access. I walked down the road when I got outside the hotel for about 5 blocks. I passed a few overpriced clothing shops. I would have to find some form of discount clothing shop. I needed things; I just wouldn't buy underwear from there. There was a salon a half a block away, Trina's. I made it to the door and inhaled deeply. This was going to hurt. I walked inside. It was time to find Katherine and start this new life.

The Dove

When I left the clothing store I went to look for a place to eat. I was hungry and I wanted coffee. I went about 4 blocks. There was a place that caught my attention. I told myself that I would get a tattoo. I went to the door and went in. there was a bald guy with a tattoo on the side of his head. This was the new Katherine. I had been out all day. I had a forged piece of paper that said my name was Katherine Rose. I was 18 and I was old enough to be here. The date on the paper was from today. There was even a seal on the piece of paper as well. Louie said that the plastic one would be ready later tonight. I walked in further, set my clothing bags down, and walked up to the counter.

"I would like a dove tattoo on my forearm."

He looked up at me. "You look like your 16, sweet thing." I smiled.

"I'm 18," he pointed to the sign on the wall. No ID No Ink... I pulled the paper out of my pocket. "Here." He ran his finger over the seal and held it up to the light.

"Looks legit. I'll get you the forms." He grabbed a book off the counter. "Pick one. I'll get the room set up after you finish your paper work." I made short work of it and signed my new name. I handed it back to him. He looked it over. "I'll go set up this is your first tattoo?"

"Yes sir."

"Your forearm huh?"

"Yes sir."

"Ok as long as you're sure." He took me back to the room. He sat me down and got all the supplies out.

"How long is this going to take?"

"Detail design and I'm guessing you want color in the olive branch?"

"Yes that would be nice."

"About an hour and a half. Maybe two."

"How much?"

"About $200 and your number." I smiled.

"How about you give me yours and I'll call you when I get my new phone set up?" He went to hand me a business card.

"Here you go, Red." He slipped it down the front of my shirt and smiled slickly. He picked the needle up and got to work. I sat back and waited.

Abduction

I was headed home from the diner after 11pm. Home... that was funny... The hotel was my home. I had tucked my tips for the night in my bra. I wasn't walking six blocks with a wad of cash just sitting in my pocket. There was a girl who was mugged a week ago. The cook at the diner told me to make sure I was careful. Be safe Katherine, he said. He liked me. I tipped him $10 every night. He told me I didn't need to, but he had kids and gas wasn't cheap. He worked two jobs so his wife could work one. He said that it was better if she was home with them for homework and making sure they ate a good dinner. The $10, though it wasn't much, made a small difference in his gas tank. He smiled at me. My orders were always right. I couldn't complain. When I got back to the hotel room I was going to count my money. I made a $150 tonight. I made $200 the night before. I was going to take that money down to Annabelle's sweet smiling smug face in the morning and pay another weeks rent on my room. I heard a whistle about two blocks away from the restaurant. I wanted to turn around and look. But something said no walk faster. The whistle came again. I went by the corner store I bought bleach from when I first got here. Someone came out from around the corner and grabbed me. I screamed but at 11pm at night who was going to hear me? It wasn't a busy night in the city either. The streets were dead. People who had come into the diner were regulars who had gotten off work to have supper. I hadn't made any friends yet. There was no one who would have done this as a prank. They dragged me kicking and screaming down the alley way.

"Let go of me you piece of shit!" There were two sets of feet they stopped. A hand slapped me.

"Shut up you little bitch." I didn't know the voice. I struggled to try and break myself free. He smacked me harder. I went slack. He picked me up more. I heard an engine start. The doors opened. He picked me up and threw me inside. There was another person in the back. They found my face with a rag. The first two people got in and held my hands down. I tried to hold my breath a long as I could before the chemicals on the rag took over. I was out cold. I didn't wake up again for a while. When I did it was dark. There was a mattress and I was cuffed to an end stand next to it. The end stand was bolted down to the floor so there was no way I could even wriggle myself out of it. I screamed. There was a voice that came out of the corner.

"Shut up you stupid bitch. There's no one around here who cares enough to hear you. If you think there's a way out of here your wrong. I welcome you to try but I will subdue you again and make you sleep. There can be good things about being here if you behave. If you refuse you will be taken care of." I swallowed.

"I need water." He walked out of the corner and slapped me.

"You will say please."

"Whatever you drugged me with made my throat dry as hell." He handed me a bottle of water. I put it in my hand that was cuffed and opened it with my free hand. Switching back hands I drank half the bottle set it down for a moment.

"Why did you grab me?" I asked.

He just laughed. "Little girl because you were needed for a great cause."

"Great cause?" He didn't answer. He got up and left the room. I heard a lock. There weren't any windows in here so I couldn't see where I was. I was cuffed so I had to stop and realize I was screwed. With my free hand I checked my bra. My ID and money were gone. I checked my pants pocket. My phone was gone too. Not that I could have called anyone. Who would come to my rescue? The cook from the restaurant? Maybe. Doubtful though. He might have called the cops. I didn't know where I was so there was no good that would have done. I checked my other pocket. My lighter and cigarettes were there. There was a small struggle getting them out of my pocket. One handed I opened the pack took a finger to raise a cigarette out and put it in my mouth. I closed the pack and set it down so I had a free hand to light the cigarette. I inhaled deeply and took another look at my surroundings. I was in no question screwed. There was no way out. I inhaled deeper on the next few drags to keep myself from freaking out. This was bad. I just got out of jail a few weeks ago. I killed two people and ran for my life. I didn't know anything about my captors. They could turn me in. What the fuck was I going to do? I got another cigarette out and lit it from the one I was smoking. I stubbed the old one out with my shoe. I inhaled deeply and exhaled on the second one. I looked at the pack with my free hand. There was over half a pack of cigarettes left. That wasn't a bad thing. Since I didn't know when I was going to get more cigarettes. I had to push my short hair out of my face. It was hard to smoke and do this at the same time. I put the cigarette in my cuffed hand, reached up, and pushed my hair out of the way. They took my hair clip out of my hair as well. What the fuck where they afraid of? Did they think I was going to swallow it and kill myself? I'm being paranoid again. I needed to slow my breathing down before I went into a panic attack. How did the shrink in jail show me how to do it again? The last thing I needed was a panic attack. I closed my eyes and started to breathe slowly. Inhale 54321 exhales 12345. This wasn't helping much. I tried to lay down flat thinking that would help some but it didn't. It wasn't completely flat. My arm was stretched out from the hand cuff in an uncomfortable manner. It was cuffed upright against the end table post. Even if I tried the fetal position it wouldn't help. I

130

sat myself upright again so I could see the door. What would this asshole do if I kicked him when he came back in? I'd have to wait to find out. I knew there were at least three of them. I heard two voices as they stuck that rag over my face and sent me to sleep for how many hours now. I stopped for a few moments. I had to think. I tried the cuff again. I folded my hand over to see if it would shimmy through the cuff. They had thought of that too. My wrists were small and they had tightened the cuff so I couldn't wriggle out. It was hard to even try. I didn't scrape it across my knuckles I didn't need to bleed with no help to fix it but I wanted to get free. Nothing. There was a sound at the door. I heard keys. The lock on the door clicked. The door opened and the man came in.

"Your name is Katherine. You work for me now. Tonight you will learn about your job and what you will be doing over your time here." He had a cup of water in his hand while he looked at me. He took a sip. My throat was dry. I wished that he would give me the cup. I shouldn't have smoked that second cigarette. It gave me cotton mouth. What am I going to be doing? I shuddered that. For having killed two men and completely on the run, I had to admit to myself that I was scared. This asshole and his friends had taken me during the middle of the night. They drugged me. Handcuffed me. Slapped me around. I didn't like being scared. It was like my mother was being slapped around. Of course there when I was panicked I had something to defend myself with and her. She was gone now. My heart hurt that she started off by lying on the stand that day. She lived in fear constantly. Maybe I shouldn't be that hard on her. I didn't have a choice on my feelings for her right now. She, in some aspects, was just as much of a liar as he was. There was nothing in there that I could use to defend myself. The man spoke again. The piece of shit told me he would be back. He was going to get me some water. He left. I looked around again. There's nothing in here. Nothing sharp I could even try to dig a spring out of the mattress to claw at him. I heard the door again. He came back with water. I'd regret the glass of water. It was laced. The room got fuzzy again.

"Your name is Katherine."

"Yes."

"You work for me. I work for you."

He said "Yes. You're going to go out on dates with men. They will ask things of you. You will do them. I'm going to show you what they will ask of you." He reached over when I couldn't fight him anymore or resist. He cuffed my free hand so as to make sure I wouldn't be able to fight back if the drugs wore off. He pulled the zipper down on my pants then jerked them down around my ankles. He lifted my shirt and tore off my bra. Without another thought he got on top of me. I tried to kick him off but he outweighed me. The next two hours were the most grueling. It was worse than smelling piss the first two weeks in jail. He had three other men come in and repeat the process. When they were done I threw up and laid there in a ball. He was still there. In the dark corner. I looked at him.

"I will repay you for this."

He got up and bent down to look at me. He grabbed my face, "You whore. You belong to me. What I say goes. If you don't like it your exit can be arranged."

The Whore House

Another night in this hell hole... The man came in again with a new dress and told me to put it on. There was an important client coming.

"Don't cry Rosie, you're going to make your big debut tonight. I did cry though. He slapped me hard. Maybe tonight he thought it was going to shut me up. Which it did, it made me hate him more as well. He had raped me and after that he had his men rape me. It was to get me ready he told me. The slimy cock sucker told me I was a whore. He told me that I would only ever be a whore. The last man slapped me around and made me bleed. I couldn't walk for two days after.

They waited for my wounds to heal before they made me dress up in this tiny red dress. One of the girls there sat me down and did my makeup. Another sat me down and did my hair. The third girl handed me a pill. She told me here take this, you won't feel a thing. One of her friends laughed and said you might not remember anything. She laughed and handed me a small cup of vodka to wash it down. I almost gagged at the smell it was so cheap. She put the pill in my hand and told me if the vodka smelled too bad to pinch my nose while I knocked some back. I started to cry again. The girl who did my makeup yelled at me that she was going to have to fix it. I stopped I told her I was sorry I just wanted to go home. She nodded she said that wasn't possible we were all stuck here.

A little time had passed; my makeup was set my hair was curled. He came back to get me. He took me to another room. I was told to sit down in the chair and wait. There was a bed in the room with two night stands. There weren't any windows to get in and out of the room. I was stuck. There was only one extra door in the room and a video camera in the room with a red light blinking. That wasn't a good sign it meant I was being watched. They recorded everything that went on in here.

Maybe they kept the footage if there was someone who was important who strolled in here so they could blackmail them. I sat and waited for about 20 more minutes. The door finally opened. In walked the jackass who had raped me first.

"Your date for the night is going to come in the room in five minutes. Get up, put the sweetest look on your face, fluff your hair, and little Katherine I can see what you're doing so you better make this the best goddamn date of your life. Whatever the man says goes. If he tells you to get on your knees you will do so. Now be a good girl and fluff your hair. Remember this Katherine if you refuse anything that's asked of you tonight. There will be hell to pay when your date leaves."

"Even if he cuts me? Beats me with whips?"

"We can see what he's doing Katherine. As long as you aren't being brutalized you will do what you're told. After he leaves I will come back and get you. Remember if you want to sleep comfortably tonight do as you're told." I straightened up in my chair. He was serious. I didn't need any more bruises. He left when I sat up. Smile Rosie. You need to smile and fake it as much as you can. The door opened and the client came in. Smile Rose its show time.

Leaving the Brothel

The night I left the brothel was a bad one. I didn't think I was going to make it out alive. He, Alex, as he called himself, had one too many vodka tonics. He passed out in my room while he was waiting for me to come back from one of my dates. Maybe come back was the wrong word. Maybe it was too strong. Considering I was only a few doors down. I had to wonder if he was there to beat me or if the client had said something bad about me when I left. But he was asleep as well. The jack ass had gotten off once after drinking a lot. He didn't make me do anything disgusting this time. When I was walked back to my room by the goon squad guard he didn't lock the door behind me. I thought that was weird but I didn't know he was in there. I felt like I needed to wake him up but I didn't. I just waited. His pack of cigarettes was on the table. I helped myself to one. Thankfully, his lighter was there too. I lit the cigarette, sat down, and took a long drag. There was a cup next to his drink with ashes in it. I ashed in there. I thought for a moment I could leave now but if I didn't make a mess he would come after me. He and his idiot goons who beat the shit out of me when I first got here. They would come after me and beat me again. They said I needed to learn who was in charge. I learned they liked to leave bruises and cut marks all over my flesh. They didn't burn me with their cigarettes thankfully. That was before they raped me. Now I was here. Night after night date after date threat after threat. Why was he in here? I was almost done with my cigarette. I put the cigarette out in the cup with the ashes. I took my shoes off and went to take off this whorish dress. If I stayed here I would have to wait until morning to take a shower. The client was truly a dirt bag; I wished the shower was now. But with this one here depending on

135

how long he stayed it wouldn't happen. He was a pig when he came for room visits. He wanted service. Usually though, it wasn't right after a date. I went to the pillow on the bed. I still had my dress on. I fluffed it up I pretended to lay down in case he was faking being asleep. I felt my hand inside the pillow among the stuffing. The baggie was still there. Some of the pills they had forced me to take were in there. Over time I had crushed some of them up and hid them inside of one of my date's coke baggies. The date thought it would be cute to do lines off of my stomach while he had me watch. He was a fat slob. He was so out of it when I palmed his baggie and stuck it in my bra. He tried to get me to take a hit. I tried a line now and then, but I didn't like where it took me. I had no self-control. I took that and I wanted to dance on stairs. I tried flying off of a banister when my date walked me down stairs. That got me confined to my room for a week and a beating. The client was told that I had a bad reaction to the drugs. I really needed time to heal from the black and blues that the goon left on me from his hands and his belt. It was like it was my fault. I was high as a kite and he had told me to make the client happy.

He didn't ask, he just slammed me around for trying to fly. When I did it the client laughed. He was high but he laughed. He told me I was a pretty bird. That pretty birds needed to fly. The client was charged double which he bitched about. I was on bed rest for two weeks. No more drugs Katie. The pig called me Katie. If I laughed about it he would have figured it out that wasn't my real name. I know that, and this pen and paper does as well. While I was there no one else needed to know. They could use that if I ever made problems for them.

He hadn't moved in a while. I went in the pillow again. I got the bag with the pill powder in. there was a pretty decent size amount of powder on the bottom of the bag; he had a drink next to him. If he was awake by now he would have betrayed himself. He wasn't that slick, he knew how to use rods and sticks and belts to instill fear. If he was awake he would have seen what I was up to. He more than likely would have killed me or badly bruised media got off the bed and went to the table where he was sleeping. I picked up his drink with a pretty decent sized pinch of powder in my hand and turned my back like I was going to take a drink. I put the dusted up pill pinch in the drink and swirled it around with my finger. I made sure there was no residue on the sides of the glass with my finger. I turned back around sat the drink down with my dry hand I wiped my mouth. It was time to wake him up. I rubbed his leg gently. He didn't budge. I massaged his leg. He coughed opened his eyes and looked at me.

He looked at his beer cup. "You helped yourself." He saw an extra cigarette butt in the cup as well.

"Yes I was thirsty after the dirt bag you set me up with tonight. You know I don't like him. He's the reason I got those bruises." He looked at me. "You need to be careful, Katie. That mouth of yours will get you more bruises. "He was quiet for a few moments, he took a drink. "You should take off your pretty dress Katie, you have another date tomorrow." I looked at him.

"You want me to wear a dirty dress? That's almost as bad as wearing dirty underwear."

"You're pushing buttons young lady." That was his phrase to let me know that he was close to wanting to beat me. He took another drink of his beer. He took a cigarette out of his pack and picked up his lighter. "I thought that would shut you up. Take a drink." He held out his cup.

"No thank you one drink was enough to wet my throat when I came back. I could use another cigarette. You can give me a kiss for it. I kissed him on the cheek. After that I picked up his pack and lighter. I lit myself another cigarette. One of these days girl you will give me a kiss and you will mean it.

I just smiled and curled up in the chair next to the table. He took another drink of his beer. It was going to take a few more moments for the dust to kick in. I hoped it would paralyze him. I didn't really know how much of what I gave. I couldn't remember how many pills were mixed in there. Thankfully he didn't have any weapons with him to try anything. If he did I think I would have had a little fun with a knife and his body parts. Mind you I've been here for two years. I'm twenty now. Two years worth of whoring. Drugs. Sleeping with countless dates. Barely eating. I was thin again from lack of sleep. They didn't seem to care. I don't think anyone there really understood that you needed to sleep and eat real food. Not just bread butter and water. Occasionally a piece of fruit or meat. Small portions so all the girls had food. They had to charge at least $300 a date so I don't know why they didn't feed us more.

He spoke again and interrupted my thoughts. "You need a new dress little Katie." He started to slur his words some. He licked his lips. That's a good beer he slurred his words when he said it. "Come here little Katie." I got up. "Come closer to me." I got close. "Take your dress off I want to look at you. I need to make sure your date didn't leave any marks on you. You have a new date tomorrow night. Someone brand new for you. That should make you happy. He's a skinny man. Nothing like what you call your other dates. You call them fat fucks when you get back here. I know the guards who work for me tell me everything. They tell me that you call me a fucking idiot little Katie. They tell me you call me a cheap bastard. Maybe you're right. I am a cheap bastard. But you don't give me a reason to spend extra on you. You don't please me. You talk like you know what's going on. All your good for is pleasing men. That's it. Maybe I should just take what I want from you like I did when you first came here when you were a virgin. Would you like that? That's the only way you're going to realize who's in charge here... and that's me." He went to get up and fell back in his chair. He looked at me. "I can't get up." I just stared at him.

I smiled and spoke. "It doesn't feel so good does it?" I walked back over to my pillow and reached into it with my hand. I pulled out the bag with the pills." You see jackass I saved almost all of the pills you tried to force down my throat. Now I'm going to force

138

them down yours while I watch as your body takes hold of the drugs." I looked him in the eyes. He looked scared for once. "You can scream. But they aren't going to come to your rescue. Not tonight. You need to understand the girls here don't like you. But your men like them. They like them more when you aren't forcing them to do evil things to their bodies. So each and every one of your goons is being occupied right now." His eyes got wide." Take another drink of your beer asshole. You're going to need it to swallow that pill."

"No..." he was begging.

"It doesn't feel so good does it? Can you imagine how I felt when you did that to me? When you drugged me and dragged me into a van? A drug soaked rag pressed to my face which knocked me out. What if we were to do that to you? What about to one of your goons? Drug you up drag you in here and bring in countless random women in here to fuck you. Would you want to be cuffed and then slapped around?" He shook his head and tried to say no, but the powder pills had kicked in enough to rid him of his speech. I took one of the whole pills from the bag and walked over to him. I picked up his drink held it to his mouth and said drink. He looked at me. "Open your mouth asshole. You're going to learn what it's like to endure the same pain you caused us. If I have to open your mouth for you it will be that much worse." He opened his mouth with what looked like a lot of effort. I took his beer and poured some down his throat then put the pill in. now swallow. He made a gulping sound when he swallowed the pill. His eyes were wide with fear. "Now asshole should I tie you up like you did to me?"

I walked over to my drawer and got my clothes out. They were worn but they were mine. That was the only thing I wanted from this hell hole and I was taking them with me. I got dressed in the Van Halen shirt that almost hung off me I was so thin. My shorts were very loose around my waist. I looked at him. "I'm surprised you didn't throw these away after having me here for two years. What were you hoping that they would kill me one of these nights and you would put me in my own things and dump me somewhere. Maybe in a ditch or a trash can in an alley. Does that sound about right? Here's what I am going to tell you. All eight girls myself included are going to drug your goons just like you and we're leaving here tonight. This place is going to burn with all of you in it." I walked over to his chair bent down to look him square in the eyes. "You and your goons make nine. All nine of you goons are going to burn tonight." He just looked at me whatever I had given him was taking strong hold of his system. "That's right Alex. Pretty soon I'm going to walk out of here and take my life back." I had to explain what was going to happen to him again since he was drugged. "But tonight Alex before I do that I'm going to kill you and your men. You need to know something. You and your men won't be the first people I've killed either. This will put the total at eleven. It won't hurt me to kill you. It won't make me cry. It's going to bring me something I take pleasure in. watching this place burn after will make the pain that you caused me slowly dissipate away. Every girl here is going to move past what you did to them. You and your sick fantasies." He just stared in sheer horror.

"Noooooo..." he stammered.

"No you fucking piece of shit no." I raised my voice. I bent down and took his shoe off. "No, you want to see no?" I took his shoe and slammed it across his face with the heel. "Here's no for every time you hit me over the last two years." I slammed the shoe again across his nose. His head went back. With how drugged up he was he tried to lift his arms and failed. When I looked at his face he had blood dripping out of his nose and down his mouth. He shed a small tear which trickled down the side of his face. I had to smile. I went over to the closet and got my sneakers out. I put them on in front of him. When I was done I started to pick through his pockets to get his office keys. He had them in his right pants pocket.

Once they were in my pocket I sat down on the bed in front of him. I took another cigarette out of his pack took his matches from the table that he left in here for nights before. Pulled one out of the pack and folded the flap back tucking the match in between the cover pulled and lit the match. I pressed it against the tip of my cigarette and inhaled to light it. I shook the match to put the flame out. I took a few drags and sat in silence. "Alex what do you think I should do with you. Do you think I should just kill you off? Leave you in a broken car? Or in an alley? Just like you did to some of the other girls here. Maybe I should take this cigarette to some of your arm flesh like you wanted to do to me when you said I wasn't behaving. I think that would be fun." I stood while I was thinking about it. I stood over him rolled his sleeves up. "Let's see how it feels Alex. So when they find your body they can see how badly you were tortured." I looked down at his wrist to see the time. The girls should be done soon I thought. So perhaps a little torture wouldn't be a good idea. I took my cigarette out of my mouth. On second thought perhaps just to scare him, I'd touch the tip of the cigarette to his skin. Yes I took my hand and rolled his arm over so the inside was exposed. I took the cigarette between my thumb and pointer finger brought it down on his arm. He made a sound like he wanted to scream. He couldn't quite figure out the right vocal chords. I laughed. "That hurt didn't it?" Another tear trickled down the side of his face.

I took the keys that I had fished from his pocket. I looked at the time. It was close to 11pm, it was time to get the hell out of here. I opened my room door turned to look at the shit hole I had lived in for the last two years. Good bye hell hole. I won't miss you. I turned back to start walking out the door. One last thought occurred to me. I turned around and kicked the chair hard that he sat in. I'm skinny mind you but my kick packed some power. He fell over. Bye you piece of shit. I ran down the hall to a door that wasn't labeled. It was shut. There was a key lock like the rest of the doors. Let's try the keys. I slipped a gold key into the lock. Turned it and felt it unlock. The door opened. It was his office. I was in luck. The office itself was a mess. I didn't know how he expected to have clients in here. Maybe this was his back office. There was a safe. What the hell was the code? I didn't have time to go back and get it out of him. He was too drugged to tell me what it was by now. His lackey came into the office. The only lackey who was left without a girl. He looked at me. I grabbed a chair and beat him with it. When he was down I hit him again and again. He stopped moving. I went over to his desk there was a shitty chair. It was ripped brown leather it looked like it needed to be bleached or just burned. This room looked like it hadn't been cleaned in a year. There was dust all over the things on top of the desk; maybe he only came back here to put money in the safe and go. I opened the drawers. There were some papers in there. Some paper clips a rubber stamp and some envelopes. I put my hand under the drawer to see if there was anything stuck under there. I could feel some tape. I bent down to see what it was. There were numbers on a piece of paper attached to the tape. There was a set of three numbers. I detached the paper went to the safe to dial in the combo. It worked thankfully. Inside the safe there were two shelves. On the top shelf there was a stack of ID's. The top of which was mine. I grabbed them. There was also one stack of hundreds banded together as well as multiple stacks of smaller bills banded together. I grabbed them all everything I could see that was in there that was cash. I got up looked for a bag. I had a wad of cash and the girls ID's and didn't have any pockets large enough to get all that money out of here. I looked around the filth hole of the office. There had to be a bag. There was. There was a crappy backpack. It would work for what I needed. I threw all the cash in there as well as the ID's and strapped it on my back. In his safe I looked one more time. There was a small .22 caliber hand gun in there with a loaded clip sitting next to it on the bottom shelf. I grabbed that too and threw it in my backpack. This was only for protection if I ran into any problems on my way back to St. Louis. I looked around the office to see if there was anything else I needed to grab. There weren't objects in an eagle eyes view that I could see needing. I walked out of the office leaving the door open. I needed to get the girls. On the way out I noticed the utility closet. It was four doors down from the office. That was perfect. There had to be something. Maybe some cleaning chemicals that was flammable. I had grabbed his cigarettes and matches from the table. There was paint thinner, Windex, bleach, paper towels, and scrub brushes. The paint thinner read flammable. I grabbed that and some paper towels. That would work. I started down the hall more to the girl's rooms. I knocked on Mari's door. She opened it; she had been waiting to go get the others.

"Go and meet outside I'm going to light this place up. You have five minutes." She had sneakers on, she was ready. I went back down the hall to his office opened the paint thinner bunched up some of the paper towels poured it on starting to drop them in various spots around the halls. Mari had made sure not to shut the doors behind her as she got each girl out. I threw a paint thinner soaked rag in each room. The pack of matches was semi full. There were eight rooms and his office that needed to be set on fire. I went back down the hall one last time and started at his office since the rag had landed on his lackey it wasn't hard to make sure the match landed there either. I went to my room and dropped the lit match on Alex and kept moving to each door. When I was down to the end of the hall way the flames were really starting to spike. I tossed the can in the flames of the last room and out the door I went I ran to the girls lets go I let out enough paint thinner soaked rags and matches to make this place blow up like the fourth of July. Mari picked up Dee and we ran up the hill behind the building.

"I'm so tired Katie can we stop?" One of the other girls had asked this.

"When we're in the clear. Do you want to die tonight? There are 9 people burning in that building. Do we want to make the count higher? I told you girls I would get you out of here. Now shut the fuck up and run." The girls went as fast as they could. We made it to the top of the hill and what looked like a safe area. There would be no chance of any rubble from an explosion hitting us. All the girls sat down. I had to turn around and stand there and watch it. I couldn't help but smile. It was done and we were free.

The Building Burned

I stood there on the hill watching the building I had lived in for the last two years burn. There were some mixed feelings about it. I thought about just leaving right now and heading back to St. Louis and collecting my things. The gun I had to begin with was in storage. There were no papers that had been in the room I had about the gun. I had used the fake address on my ID that was now backing in my pocket. The gun was probably gone my things were probably sold. Why would I think it would be there still? Not that I thought anyone from the diner would have collected it. The cook no less if he took home young girl items I think his wife would have probably freaked out. I can't say that I would blame her. Before the night began the girls and I agreed that we would make sure that we were in our street clothes. Not the date dresses. There were eight of us. We all looked like we came out of a prison camp. Dee Dee, if that was her real name, looked the worst out of all of us. She was literally skin and bones. She had hard time breathing when we went up the hill to escape the fire. Mari and I had to take turns pretty much carrying her. I got them out. I smiled to myself as I write this, I remember that day. I saved lives. Not as many as I had taken but I gave a little back. I turned and looked at them. "Go home ladies. Get as far and fast away from here as possible."

"But" Mari asked "What are we going to do for money? How are we going to get there? And for that matter where the hell are we to begin with?"

"Money I can give you. I raided Alex's safe before I came to get you girls. Your ID's were in there as well. It looks like he kept

144

everything we had on us minus our phones because they were traceable if they were left on. So there's no GPS there's not a lot of street signs to see where the nearest police station is. But once I get you girls there or even to the hospital I'm leaving and going back home to St. Louis. Both of my parents are long gone. There are no brothers and sisters that are worried about me."

Mari looked at me wide eyed. "You don't want to report what happened to you?"

"Why? Who's going to believe me? I'm basically a 20 year old orphan who was kidnapped, molested, drugged and had her body sold for sex. You girls are more important. Let's get you to where you can get some help and we need to get her medical attention." I pointed to Dee Dee. I looked over at her. She looked pitiful. She was fighting to breathe. She had a nasty bruise on her leg as well. The client she saw on a regular basis had a penchant for tying her up and beating her. She smiled once and said she enjoyed it. I told her she was a liar. She didn't talk to me for two weeks after that. I just shrugged it off. That was shortly before Alex decided to separate us girls from really spending time with each other. Even now I count my stars that they never figured out who I really was even after my hair grew out. I was going to rent out a room to take the longest hottest shower ever. After that I would take myself to a beauty shop. I needed to get my hair back to where it was the night that they took me. Dee Dee looked at me.

"You look like you saw a ghost right now Katie."

"I think I did. Maybe it was just a ghost of my former self. I'll tell you this much. I'm going to get that girl back and she's coming back with a vengeance." The girls were wide eyed and looked at me funny.

"Don't you feel anything? You just lit the building on fire while those men were in there burning."

"Why would I feel anything about them? They beat us. They raped us and treated us like we were just property for sale. Don't you remember Ki? Don't you ever wonder what happened to her? "Sasha looked up. She was Ki's best friend.

"Yea I missed her after she left. Alex told us she went with one of the clients."

"No she didn't because I got Ki's client after she was gone. The client got her so coked out that she had a heart attack. They put her back in her street clothes. Took her outside and left her for dead."

Karla's eyes got really wide when she turned around. "Do you mean to tell me that we all would have ended up like that?"

"Yes to them we were expendable."

"Katie what's in your backpack?"

Your ID's and cash that I lifted from the safe in Alex's office. I told you before I would give you money. He left the code taped under the desk in his office. I guess he needed a reminder card with all the drinking he did. But he never let anyone in his back office. It was a sty. Not even his goons were in there. Just him. I'm not kidding ladies the office was terrible and dirty just like him. It made our rooms like hospital clean." One thing I didn't write down before was that the comforter in my room was stained badly with bodily fluid that wasn't my own. He let me wash it after I spent a week of sleeping on the floor. I left the pillow in the dryer for an hour. I didn't care that it ruined the pillow. I burned out whatever germs from the previous room owner might have had. I knew I was going to get a STD check as well. I had no idea where a clinic would be before I made it to my final stop on getting the life I was making for myself back in order. They started looking at me funny. Maybe I paused for too long. "Ok we don't have any phones with us I told them. So we need to go on foot. It's going to take some time with this one," looking at Dee Dee. She gave me a dirty look. Look I realize I wasn't very nice but we need to get you medical attention. She nodded still looking butt hurt. I think she realized I wasn't kidding she was a mess. "Let's go. We need to see if we can find a store. Maybe a payphone for a cab. You girls we need to figure out who can take turns to help carry Dee Dee so we can get there. When we find a store maybe they will break a twenty so we can get change and I can call a cab to get us all to the hospital. Like I told you before once I get you there I am leaving. Before we get moving I'm going to count out the money I took from the safe." I knew there was at least 3,000 in small bills and 10k in large. If I gave them each $800 and their ID's I would have $6600 to start over with left over. Maybe I'm selfish but I didn't have to save their lives. Call it a finder's fee.

I have no intention of helping them more after I got them to the hospital. Even if they begged I was gone. Let's get her ready. I zipped up the back pack and put it on my back. Mari helped Dee Dee up. I went over to the both of them. I was a bit taller than Dee Dee so I bent down for her to put an arm around my neck. That wasn't going to work. She was 5'2 and Mari was closer to my height. We wrapped our arms around Dee Dee's to steady her. There were buildings around us. "Let's go.We have a while to go and one of you girls doesn't have shoes on so we have to be careful about where we walk. Let's go." It was about thirty minutes of walking. We saw a small store. "Let's go inside there maybe they will let us call a cab from their phone."

Dee Dee looked at me. She said she hoped they have a place to sit down." I don't feel so good." She was wheezing a lot. I had to wonder if she had asthma from all the coke they made her do. But I was no nurse. So I was probably wrong. Maybe they didn't make her do it at all. Maybe she wanted it. Maybe I shouldn't have saved her. The others probably would have crucified me if I hadn't. I needed to put that out of my head. Or I would fuck myself on getting to my destination. There didn't need to be more guessing and second guessing myself.

I walked into the store. Mari followed behind me. She grabbed my arm. "There's real food in here. And junk food. I could eat myself to death."

"Let's get some juice for everyone. That's something healthy that we haven't and they haven't had in a long time" I said. The clerk behind the counter looked at us both funny like we were going to cause problems. I grabbed eight bottles of orange juice from the cooler and some small cookies. I was sure Dee Dee would crash soon so the sugar would help her. Mari and I walked up to the counter. He looked at me like he was going to ask how I was going to pay for everything. I opened the bag and took out a wad of small bills. How much I smiled at him. He kind of jumped. Like he was expecting something else. What, I don't know. But that was beside the point. He had one of those registers that you had to key everything in by hand. I really didn't care. As long as I got the food. I handed him the cash and he bagged it up. He handed me the change. I gave the bag to Mari. Go give this to the girls. She nodded and went outside.

He asked me was there something else I needed. "Yea. Can I use your phone? I need to call a cab. I need to get all of us to a hospital."

"You're kidding me right?"

"Why would I be kidding? I was held captive for the last two years of my life and treated like a sex slave. I'm tired I'm hungry. I have seven other girls who are just as badly damaged if not worse than I am. So yes I need to use your phone so we can be on our way. I really don't think you want to have to call the police for loitering girls do you? I'm asking you to help us. Rather than make our night even harder since we escaped by the skin of our teeth." He looked at me funny. "And before you get any silly ideas. I'm not easy and I have a bad temper. So be a good citizen and help us. "He looked at me like I was threatening him. I smiled sweetly or as sweetly as I could remember how to. "I'm smaller than you dude.

And I don't have any weapons just cash. Do you need an extra dollar or two for the phone call?" I took my bag off my back again went to dig some more money out.

He spoke up and said "Stop." He got his phone out and started dialing. While the phone rang he just looked then asked if the rest of the girls wanted to come inside while we waited. The phone rang again. He had his cell phone on speaker. "There's no one that's going to follow you is there? Aside from you all I don't want any trouble or drama tonight." I smiled again.

"No." He didn't have a name tag on so I couldn't use his name. "There's no one that followed us here. And there won't be anyone coming out of where we left. I set the building on fire when I got the little one out." I pointed out the window at Dee Dee. Mari was helping her sit down on the curb so she could eat.

The cab company picked up the phone. He gave the order and said that it would be better if there was a van. There were a lot of us. He made sure to tell them we were all sober. We needed medical attention. He hung up. "You can bring your friends inside."

"Ok but you're helping the little one get off the curb. And she needs time don't get your patience lost. It took a half hour to walk here with her." He nodded slowly.

"What did they do to her?"

"You don't want to know. Imagine the worst kind of torture that people view as pleasure and there's your answer." His mouth dropped. "This is mean but close your mouth and follow me if you really want to help. Be a gentleman if you know how and lets go pick her up and bring the rest of them inside."

"We can lock the door until the cab gets here if you want," he said. "If that will make you feel safer."

149

"You can ask them. Nothing personally is going to make me feel safer than getting the fuck out of here and away from this Podunk." He just looked at me strangely. But I couldn't deny it. He went to the door while I adjusted the bag back on my shoulders. I walked over to the door and he opened it politely. "Thank you. Ladies Vincent here has offered us all to stand inside and wait until the cab comes. He was even gracious enough to tell them that we needed a van. Dee he's going to help you up. So you can get inside to wait there with everyone." She nodded. He kept his word and was polite. He helped her up and walked inside. After Dee Dee was inside the others walked in as well. Mari whispered to me that I made quick work of his attitude.

"You think?"

She smirked. "What did you tell him?"

"The truth. It seems like that would be the only way to get through to him. He's not very bright and he looks like he either smoked one too many joints or he was knocked into one too many walls. He's doofy but cautious. He doesn't want the fuzz here which I can understand I don't either." Mari nodded. She was a strong solider. She was in that hell hole a year longer than I was. She told me she wanted to snap Alex's neck. A few times I told her she was too skinny. Yet I was two sizes smaller.

How long did they say it would be before the cab would be here? We were all safely inside. Vincent locked the door and turned the closed sign. I guess he figured that there would be a lot of trust issues so he left the keys hanging in the lock so we could get outside if we wanted. Maybe he was just a stoner who didn't want any cop problems. I can't say that I blame him. I had my own shit to worry about and getting busted by the cops was not in my cards. Dee Dee decided she was going to flirt with Vincent. She wanted a soda. I handed him a 20$ and said, "If she asks for anything else just to take it out of that. No sense in getting you in trouble. You're already risking your neck." He smiled. I had to wonder if he knew who Alex was. I hoped not. But there could be far worse things.

"Did you girls want me to turn on the TV so you have something to listen to?" I spoke up quickly.

"No thank you."

Karla just shrugged, "Maybe if you have some CD's or music?" She loved music. She had a voice on her that could have made someone cry for joy. She was a looker too. Maybe in a few years she'd get the chance at a singing career. Maybe find a husband. I was being hopeful. Ten minutes had passed. There was no cab. Vincent put on some rock music which sounded like what I listened to in high school. That was only four years ago. What had I turned into since then?

I needed to get out of here. "Do you think you could call the cab again? Maybe see where they are? Didn't they tell you when it would be here?" He said he would call them back in five more minutes. That way you can give them time for being at red lights or behind shitty drivers. He looked directly at me when he said it. I think he was getting how severe that the girls were scared to be out of there. Karla hadn't stopped looking around. She jumped when Mari touched her. I had to look over at the other Katie she was looking at the food with big eyes.

"Baby girl are you hungry?"

"I am but I want a salad and a burger. Real food that I can sink my teeth into. The food here has all the calories that will sit on my ass."

"You need some good food to sit on your ass." She laughed. Sondra was sitting on the floor looking lost. Jenna was looking out the window she turned around.

"Five minutes is over. Call them." Vincent picked up the phone and called. He put the call back on speaker phone. The cab company answered he gave the pickup address. They put him on hold. They said they needed to call the cab and find out where it was. There was a two minute delay while we waited for the service to come back on the line.

"Sir the van should be pulling up with in the next five to ten minutes. There was a delay in getting a van to accommodate all the passengers that you have waiting." Vincent said thank you and hung up. We waited five more minutes. The cab finally showed. Vincent went to unlock the door.

"Your cab is here ladies." He went to Dee Dee to help her up. I looked at my seven traveling companions. They all looked tired.

"Katie you're leaving us when we get to the hospital right?"

"Yea I'm going to get to the bus depot as soon as I get you there. The first bus out of here and back to St. Louis." Vincent looked at me.

"You can come back here. I'll take you. It's a 4 hour ride from here."

"Where are we I asked?"

"Joplin. There's a business district here." He helped Dee Dee walk outside and told the driver he needed to take us to the local hospital. The driver looked at all of us. He asked if we had a bad night. I almost laughed.

"Try like over 600 of them or more for all of us combined." The driver looked. Maybe he knew the whore house. Or he had taken clients there. Something had told me he had. Vincent came up to me as all the other girls boarded into the van. He handed me his cell phone.

"It's pre-paid so even if you don't come back I won't lose a lot of money. There's a home and work number programmed in there. You can call me later if you want. But if you run into problems you can call 911 you might need it."

"In case I don't make it back here's $60 so you can buy a new pre-paid and start a new account tonight." I had a receipt from this place in my pocket when I made it back to St. Louis I would drop it in a padded envelope and mail it back here for him. I got in the back and squished in with Jenna and Sondra. Kassidy was in the front of the cab with the driver. She had a bit of a temper. So if the driver started anything she would hit him. I took the bag off and started to count the stacks of money out into stacks of 8. Not showing them how much was in there so I still had a sizeable stash when I got to St. Louis. Maybe when I got to St. Louis and to the hotel my old friend Annabelle would be there and my clothes as well. It was a pipe dream but they were nice clothes which I had spent a minor fortune on. If I talked to the restaurant owner maybe he would let me have my job back for tips or something. I would get that back. That was normal and normal was what I needed. Hidden in the crowd faceless. The cab took us down two of the streets we walked down to get to the convenience store.

"What's the name of the hospital you're taking us to?"

"Christ Memorial ma'am."

"What street is it off of?"

"Arthur and Central." Kassidy just sat there and watched him make every turn.

"Katie I wish you weren't leaving us when we get there. You have just as much of a right to tell your story about that place as we do."

"That's ok. I just need to make sure you girls get there and I'm gone." Mari piped up, that's what she wants and we need to respect that. She had some sense about her. The conversation was dropped from there. There was a bit of silence. I was almost done with sorting the money. I had six piles of money sorted out I needed one more. I made quick work. When it was done I bundled it up with each girl's ID to pass forward. Kassidy turned around and thanked me. She didn't expect as much as I gave them. It was an even $800 for all of them. Mari was next she commented on how good it felt to have her ID back. Like it was a part of her that said who she really was. A piece of the puzzle came back into place after she had been abducted. One by one they all murmured a thank you and commented something along the lines of what Mari had said.

The driver turned to Kassidy, "We are two blocks from the hospital. You want to gather your things up. I stuffed Vincent's phone in the bag and zipped it up. He hit a red light when he was a block away. He stopped short. Are you ladies all ok?" The driver looked at Kassidy. I watched her. She didn't know what to say.

Mari piped up. "We're fine thank you." He nodded. Maybe he had some remorse. I'd never know. The light changed. And he drove he put the blinker on to turn into the hospital driveway. Mari was looking out the windows to watch for signs. I went in the bag to get some cash out to pay the tab. the meter was $63.17. I pulled a $100 out of the bag and handed it up to him. Mari told him to stop directly in front of the emergency room door so we could pile out there. He did and then got out of the cab to open the doors. He went to give me change. I told him to keep it and forget that he met us. He looked at me. He looked at Kassidy she gave him one of her dirtiest looks she could imagine. He took his money got back in the cab and drove off.

We stood outside the entry of the ER. The girls looked at me. Mari spoke up. "Well this is good bye. Katherine thank you." The girls came over and hugged me. Dee Dee looked at me and said she was sorry she then said thank you. I smiled and hugged her. I made sure the back pack was secured on my shoulders. Kassidy as I turned to walk away said that I needed to find a knife and a sandwich. I just shook my head and threw a peace sign up behind my head and walked out of the ER parking lot. I waited at the entrance where they couldn't see me so I knew they went inside. They stood there for a few moments and then looked at the door. Mari led the way as she turned to walk inside. Kassidy followed up the tail end making sure that everyone went inside. I smiled. I turned after they were in the doors completely and walked into the night.

After the Hospital

I got a couple of miles down the road. When it looked like the coast was clear I stuck my thumb out to catch a passerby's attention. Maybe they would take me to the train station or the bus depot? I didn't want to risk turning Vincent's phone on. I didn't know if he would be able to track it. It was a prepaid phone. One of the girls in prison had told me that they were the worst phones to have. Powered off was the best positon for them. I kept walking I put my head down. It felt like I was walking through that court house three years ago. Keep your head down Rose. I could still hear the lawyer. I had to stop and think about her. If I called her now three years later what would happen to me. Prison? Back to grown women hitting on me and poor prison food. It made me fat which I needed but it was terrible. Maybe it would be a luxury compared to the last two years I spent in that place. I knew one thing I didn't want to find out. I stuck my hand out again and put my thumb up to try again to hitch a ride. I counted 15 cars going by. Nothing I put my arm down again and kept walking.

I was tempted to turn Vincent's phone on to sneak a peek at the time. It wasn't worth the risk. I kept walking. There was a sign for drivers to drive with caution because of pedestrians. How considerate. Traveling down the streets more there was about a thirty minute gap. A blue car pulled up next to me. The window rolled down. Music blared. I looked at the driver. There was a female in the driver's seat. "Need a lift?"

"Yea where are you headed? About 10 miles outside St. Louis. You need a lift or what?" She was skinny. She had big boobs and her skirt was really short. You had to wonder why she was dressed that way.

"Sure I could really use the help. Get in. she unlocked the door. I opened it. The floor was a mess so was the back seat. There were spare clothes. The car smelled of weed, sex, and cigarettes. She offered me one. It had been about six hours since I had one. I was itching for one.

"Please." She handed me the pack. I opened it and took one out. "Do you have a lighter?" She fished one out of the driver's side door and handed it to me. It was a plain BIC with a pot leaf on it. She asked me where I was headed from. "Hell." She laughed.

She looked at me, "You're serious aren't you?"

"Yea kind of."

"You want something stronger than a cigarette? We can pull over and burn one." I looked at her. "What kid you haven't ever smoked a joint?" I laughed.

"I've smoked a few in my 20 years. Forcibly. So I didn't enjoy it." She looked at me and saw the cold look in my eyes.

"Whoa kid. Where did you come from?"

"The hospital. I dropped off a few people who were tortured right along with me. They needed medical attention. She just looked at me like if she looked at me long enough she might catch me in a lie." I just stared at her. I don't think that there's anything left in my soul to where she could have seen something human. Someone who cared. That someone got turned off when I left the girls at the hospital.

She just laughed. It was a scared laugh. "What's your name kid?"

"It's Katherine." I needed to keep up my name change.

"My name is Scarlet," she said. I could tell she was lying. Maybe that was her stage name. She looked like a stripper. Or a street walker. Hell maybe she was just an escort. One thing I knew was I wasn't going to get close enough to find out. She pulled off to the side of the road. She pulled out a second pack of cigarettes from the door pocket that was lined with rolled joints. She took one out it stank to high heaven. I wrinkled my nose. She looked at me like I didn't know what I was doing. "Calm down kid." She fished another BIC lighter out of the door panel and lit it. She inhaled deeply and let out a huge cloud of smoke. She leaned back in her seat. "Fuck I needed that," she said. She handed me the joint. "Inhale slowly kid. You'll enjoy it more. You aren't being forced this time." I took the joint from her and pinched it in my fingers like she had brought it to my lips and inhaled then slowly exhaled like she said to. I handed it back to her. "I told you kid. It isn't going to bite you. Don't be afraid." She took it from me and took a pair of tweezers out from the center console to grip the joint. She left enough to where she could still puff on it and not burn herself. She took another puff and sat in the driver's seat kind of limply. I had to wonder if she was going to be able to drive after this. Thankfully she didn't read my thoughts this time. She handed it back to me with the tweezers. "Take another hit kid and I won't bother you with another one." So I did. A small one. She didn't complain. I relaxed back in the car with her in my own seat. She just sat there for a while. "I'm good now I can drive."

"I don't know anything about this. But if you're sure. Alright." I stopped to think about it. I felt my upper arms to make sure my bag was still there on my back. I didn't want to be screwed again with literally no money stuck in the middle of nowhere. Almost made me want to go back to Chicago. But I had no one there. The minute I stepped foot on Chicago soil I was sure I would be arrested. My head was fuzzy from the weed. She sat there for about 30 more minutes giggling at nothing. Or what she said was nothing. Watching her was kind of ridiculous. But what could I do about it?

She looked at me a few times she asked if I wanted her to light another so I would mellow out more. I said no she just shook her head. "Kid you need to lighten up more or its going to be a long ride back to St. Louis."

I nodded. I had to agree with that. I smiled at her. I'm fine. Just out of my element. She laughed. I was out of my element five years ago. Pot helped that. She turned the keys to get the engine to start. Let's go kid. The faster we get where you're going the faster you'll lighten the fuck up. Maybe if I told her what I'd been through the last four years of my life. She would understand. or maybe she would kick me out of the car because I harshed her high.At least the sign on the side of the road we passed said that there was about 240 miles more to go. That was about 2 more hours maybe more. She picked her drink up. Maybe it would be a bit more than that. She would probably have to stop for a restroom break or two. It was one of those big gulp drinks from a gas station. She drank it like it was water. But it wasn't it looked like pop. I sat back in the seat of the car. There was a poke in my back. It brought me back to reality. I remembered that there was the .22 in the bag. The clip wasn't in the gun. But it was in the bag still. I smiled. I had a small bit of security. If she kicked me out of the car I could force my hand and make her drive the rest of the way. She's not the brightest crayon in the box.

The buzz from the two hits was wearing off. I smiled some more. I was back in control. She looked at me. "I'm guessing that high kicked in for you. You're smiling from ear to ear."

"I am? I guess I had a small moment of calm."

"Good maybe you'll relax some. There's more than three hours and we need to make the best of it." I nodded.

"You're right." We had been in the car together for about an hour.

"You know what kid I didn't introduce myself properly earlier. My name is Viv."

"Pleased to meet you again Viv. I'm Katherine. I don't always meet people like this. I never do to be honest. Scarlet sounded like a good name to give you. So I'm sorry I was dishonest with you. I'm usually a very private person when it comes to my name. I'm not offended Viv. You have to realize that when you pulled up beside me I was scared that someone who recognized me from where I came from was pulling up next to me. I would have freaked out if it was. I don't ever want to go back there." She nodded. She didn't argue.

She did ask me again though if Katherine was my real name. "Yes ma'am it is."

"So Katherine what the fuck happened to you?" I guess it was time to tell her. So I did.

"For starters I was taken two blocks away from my work. Drugged and dragged into a van while I was unconscious. Brought to a building where there were 7 other girls who were sex slaves. Taken the same as me away from life as they knew it. Beaten drugged and treated like they were property."She just looked at me like I was crazy. Like I was lying but maybe the flatness in my voice told her elsewise.

"How did you get out?"

"I saved the pills that they tried to force down my throat. Kept them hidden inside a ratty pillow that I slept with. One night when the piece of shit that ran the place came to see me. I drugged him. They all made it out. Eight of us made it out."

"But what about the men?" I just smiled. She looked at me funny.

"He and his goons won't be an issue anymore. They were a problem and it needed to be taken care of. The problem was solved."

"What did you do to them Katherine?"

"Just a taste of their own medicine. That's all." Maybe she was still high. Or maybe she was just dumb but she thought I was meaning that I got them all thrown in jail. This was the farthest thing from the truth. I think she would have kicked me out of the car by then if she knew I killed 9 men within the last 24 hours. Maybe she would have indeed forced my hand. Who knows? But she kept driving which was good. She didn't ask any more questions. Which I couldn't complain about.

About half an hour passed of just pure silence then she said, "Are you hungry?"

I told her yes. We were on a highway. "Well maybe something cheap. I have a little money but not much. I can't imagine after everything you have been through you have a lot of cash."

I shook my head. "No I don't." She didn't need to know what I stole. When it came down to it my vision on the stealing was skewed since I didn't get paid for the last two years. What I took from his safe was like pay. Not as much as I was worth or what I had given the girls to buy themselves plane tickets home with were worth. But none the less it was something to help them get home. Maybe the FBI would get involved and send them home for free. Who knew? I hoped they didn't pull my prints off of Dee Dee or for that matter any of the girl's IDs. They would know who Rose was. They would come looking for me. Maybe going past St Louis would be a good idea. But perhaps stopping by the hotel and seeing my old fat friend was there. It had been two years. I still wondered if she was there. If she had been the one who set me up to be taken. Maybe she would want to meet my gun and find out. That brassy haired cunt had to have known something. Maybe I would just shoot her to shoot her. It didn't make a difference. To me if I added one more person to the list of 11. 12 was a nice even number. Viv pulled off of the freeway and on to a side road. She went down a short road and slowed down to pull into a parking lot of a sandwich shop. They had a 2 for $5 special listed.

"Come on kid. For $10 bucks we can eat like queens and get drinks too."

I smiled." Ok."

I felt my stomach growl. It was going to be an over load but it would be worth it. When she got ready to park the car I told her I was going to eat slowly. So I didn't get sick in the car on the way back to St. Louis. She nodded

"Probably a good idea kid. I know my car's a mess but I do not want to clean up puke. Not mine and certainly not anyone else's." I just looked at her and shook my head.

"You would think that I had an eating disorder with how skinny I am."

"A forced eating disorder kid. You didn't have a choice."

"You're right about that." We went in and ordered. "Do they have coffee here?" I would die for a cup of Joe. A real one where I pour in the creamer or half and half. The kid on the other side of the counter said they had it. I looked at Viv. "Can I have a cup please? And a small turkey sandwich with easy mayo?" Viv said it wasn't a problem. Maybe she had a change of heart and realized I wasn't totally uptight.

I would need to be careful still because you wouldn't know if she was going to flip. We sat down and she watched me put the creamers in my cup and stack them. When I was done I called them the leaning tower of creamers. She laughed. "You haven't really had a chance to be a kid or grow up have you kid?"

"No not really." She drank her soda and sat there.

"Well once I drop you off I'll give you my number. We can talk if you ever need an ear." I thought to myself I would have her going hourly rate. Would that make me a lesbian? No. I would have to have sex with her in order to be a lesbian. I guess she would be like a shrink. I hoped I was smiling while I was thinking about all this.

"That sounds really good. Like a really nice idea." She smiled when I focus on her. I guess I must not have snickered or smirked. We were both almost done with our food. The small sandwich filled me up.

"You ready? Let's go." I cleaned up my wrapper and cup and followed her out. She looked at me when we got ready to get in the car.

"Are you going to take the backpack off?"

"When we get to St. Louis, yes."

"Oh I thought we were getting somewhere with trust."

"We are," I told her. My bag is just like a security blanket." She just laughed.

"I was right you really haven't had a real chance to grow up yet and be an adult. Get in. We have an hour and a half to go." When I sat down she handed me a piece of paper to put in my pocket. It was a napkin with her phone number on it. I folded it up wiggled and tucked it into my shorts pocket.

It was weird how she watched me move. Like she was afraid or she was into me. If she was afraid maybe she would kick me out. I guess I needed to be careful. I had to wonder why she was going so far from home the way she was dressed. Maybe it was my turn to grill her.

"Viv, how come you're so far from home?"

"Oh I drive a lot sometimes for work, sometimes for a rock show. I'm a model." She was pretty thin. I had to wonder what she modeled. But I wasn't going to say anything unless she offered up her info. I mentioned she was weird. She interrupted my thoughts.

"I'm going to smoke a cigarette, you want one?"

"Yes please may I?" She handed me her pack and lighter. I took one out lit it and rolled down the window. She turned on the radio. She went for a channel with pop songs to sing along to. I was just quiet. That was probably the biggest meal I had eaten in the last two years. I would probably sleep if I wasn't so nerved about being in a car with someone who I still don't know so well. I mean I was held in captivity for the last two years of my life.

She looked at me. "Do you want to smoke another doob with me?"

"Not yet I want this food to settle." She nodded.

"I know you aren't a pro kid. But it would take the edge off of your stress which is why you're having a hard time digesting your food." I told her the reason I was having a hard time was because it was the first real meal I had eaten in two years. I almost said since I had gotten out of prison. Holding off on that little fact I thought might be a good idea. She wouldn't be so nice. I've thought that many times over and over the last hour and a half that I had been with her. She thought I was a sweet little abused girl. I sat there quietly for a few moments.

"Viv may I have another cigarette?" She picked her pack up out of the door panel again. She handed it to me.

"The lighter's in the cup holder between the two of us." She handed me the pack that had the joints as well. "In case you change your mind." I smiled. I looked out the window we were 15 miles outside of St. Louis. There she would drop me off. I lit the cigarette and inhaled. I set both packs and her lighter in her cup holder.

"Thanks Viv."

"You're welcome kid. "She flipped the channels on the car stereo again. Some dark rock came on and out the speakers. Maybe this will make you feel better kid. The 10 mile marker came up. She didn't talk much accept to ask me how I was feeling from the sandwich. I told her I was alright. The real food hadn't created too much chaos on my insides. The next ten miles we listened to music in silence.

The Hotel Back in St. Louis

She dropped me off in St. Louis outside the hotel. "You have my number kid. Call me. I'll come back. We can go to dinner or some shit." She gunned the engine while she waited for me to reply.

"That sounds great." I walked back a couple of steps like I was going to leave and she said see ya, and drove off. My bag was still on my back. It was 8am Annabelle would just be getting off work. I was ready to walk in. This time I had my ID on me so I was prepared for any shit this bitch, if she was still there, would give me. Viv would get home shortly, smoke another doob and pass out. Or at least that's what I was betting. I got ready to walk to the door and took a breath and looked in the window. She was there. She looked even brassier and heavier than she did two years ago. I opened the door and walked in. She had her back turned and told me she would be right with me.

"No problem." When she was done fiddling with whatever she turned around and looked at me.

"You."

"Yes I am back. How are you sweet Annabelle?" I made sure my voice was extra syrupy sweet.

"You just left during the middle of the night and you didn't come back." She was stuttering.

"No Annabelle, I was taken off the street on my way back from work. But that's not the point. I came here to collect or inquire about my things that were here."

She looked at me. She said, "It's been two years. You think your things are still here?"

"No I don't think. I'd like to inquire if they are. If they aren't I will be on my way. But if you're going to have an attitude I'm sure your manager and I can have a chat again like we did two years ago. I don't think you want to call him and have me bitch again. I've just spent the last two years of my life as a sex slave. Locked in a building with 7 other women. I don't know if you know that but not but a few hours from here were a sex slave trade and a douche sleaze bag named Alex was in charge of it. Did you know him?" She just looked at me. "Maybe you better call your manager. I think I just want to collect my things and be gone. And please before you hit the panic button under your counter. I'm not really in the mood for a fight with the cops too. I've had a long trip in the car today with someone I don't know just to get here. There was clothing which should have tags on it. And there was money. My tip money that I earned from the diner. The money I don't care about granted it was about $500 but I can go without and make more." She picked up the phone and dialed 3 numbers. The only words she said when they picked up was I think you need to come down here. She hung up.

"The manager will be right down."

"Thank you Annabelle." She smiled. It took about 5 minutes for the manager to come down stairs. The same douche from two years ago.

"Yes Annabelle how can I help you?"

"Our guest here would like to inquire about her belongings that were left here about two years ago."

He looked at me. "You look familiar. What was your name?"

"Katherine, Katherine Rose."

"Yes I remember you now. You paid up front in cash. You weren't here for very long."

Yes that's correct. Let me see your clothes. No we don't have those anymore. They were donated to charity for battered women at our local parish. The backpack it was thrown out. There was no use for it. The money after we realized that you weren't coming back it was taken to pay off your bill. You were noticed missing about a week after. Your boss called here and asked if you had checked out. Which we told him you hadn't. We also told him we hadn't seen you. The rest which was a total of $50 was donated to the parish with your clothing. That was, mind you, after we realized you weren't coming back."

I smiled sweetly. "Sir I think it's amazing you did that. And I wouldn't kick up a fuss normally, but realize that I've been missing for the last two years. I was abducted a few blocks from here in the dead of the night. I was taken beaten and raped and sold over and over again as a sex slave. So if you wouldn't mind ever so much if I could see receipts for the donations and I'll be on my way. No fuss no attitude. I think that was the best possible donation you could have made." He went over to the desk.

"You know ordinarily we don't just show receipts miss. But and excuse me for this you look like hell. I'll make an exception this one time."

I smiled. Perhaps he had some southern boy charm. Annabelle hadn't moved. She was standing there in awe because she had seen her boss be nice to me twice. She wasn't thrilled looking at him. She shot me a very dirty look.

"Here I thought when she left the trash was gone from our hotel."

"Dear sweet Annabelle," I just looked at her. "I'd shut up if I were you. I still think you had something to do with me being taken off the street. So really just shut the fuck up so your boss can do his job and I'll be on my way."

"Miss Rose. Whereas I can appreciate your need for silence while I work. You're no longer a guest here. Please don't speak to my staff like that again or I will ask you to leave and not help you."

"You're right I apologize Annabelle. And Annabelle it would do you a bit of good to hold your tongue while we have a client here. We wouldn't want Ms. Rose leaving here and telling people how poorly you treat guests or potential guests. That would put a damper on business which would dampen your paycheck if there are no customers to pay your salary."

Her eyes widened and looked at him. Something told me she wasn't used to being hushed. They were probably fucking each other. But I would guess she wore the pants. It was almost disgusting to watch them. He looked like he was almost done thumbing through the file cabinets. "Here we go. Room 212 from two years ago." He took the file out. He walked towards the counter and me. He opened the folder on the counter and faced it my way. "Here you are Miss Rose. You can go through the papers in here and see everything for yourself." Plain as day it was all there. The cash receipts for the room bill. The charity stamps for the clothing that was in the room. All $500 dollars' worth of clothing. Clothes didn't come cheap more so when you only had two pairs to your name. The next page was for the cash. The home for women. There was a nun's name who signed for it. There was a seal to

169

show it was official as well. Seals can be forged. But when I ran a finger over it seemed real enough.

"Do you have a piece of paper? I'd like to write these addresses down." He took the papers over to the desk and took them each out and copied them quickly. He returned to the counter and placed them all in front of me. I picked them up folded them and placed them in my pocket. "Not that I disbelieve anything you say of course I really want to see these places for myself."

"Of course you do" he replied. "I would rightfully understand why after all you have been through."

I flipped to the end of the file. There was a key. Here it is. "Do you mind if I take this? That is indeed mine."

"Feel free to take it with you."

I had to smile at his false sense of graciousness, "Thank you." I smiled sweetly as sweetly as I could. I put the key in my pocket. I closed the file and handed it back to him. "Thank you that's all I need from the file. I'll be on my way now." I smiled at both of them. I left quickly not telling them that I was going to check into everything to make sure the receipts were real and the stamps as well. Annabelle and I had a date later if they weren't. A reckoning day would be upon her. I decided quickly that reckoning day would be upon her regardless. That bitch knew more than she was saying. The parish where my clothes were donated was close 3 according to the paper. That would take me about 15 minutes to walk there. I passed a cafe on the way. I would eat there later. There had to be a decent cup of coffee there. The blocks went by quickly. There was indeed a parish. I went inside. There was a nun at a desk in the office. She looked up.

"May I help you dear?"

"Yes ma'am my name is Katherine Rose. I wanted to check this receipt that was given from your parish for a donation of clothes and one for money a little over two years ago. I pulled the paper out of my pocket and handed it to her. This is a photo copy."

She took it from me. "Yes this is my signature. I took that in from the hotel. They were brand new."

"Yes ma'am they were. But I really wanted to make sure that this was a real place. The donations were made and used for people who really needed them. I've had two long years." She smiled.

"Not to fret my dear. They went to good use. The nun was so peaceful."

"Thank you and I am sorry for your hardship you had to endure over the last two years. It will get better for you I am certain."

I smiled. "Thank you sister for your kindness it means so much."

"You're welcome." I got ready to leave. The nuns said, "Go in peace child." I smiled. She went back to work. I left. I needed to find Annabelle. She should be on her way home. She didn't drive two years ago. Maybe that was still the same. I double backed to the hotel and watched her leave. She went a block. I stayed behind her. She still didn't have a car. Her place wasn't far. I watched her cross the street from a block behind. She went to a brownstone and dug her keys out. She had one of those huge purses. The ones that women carried for fashion status statements. I stopped while she dug for her keys flipped my bag around zipped it open and put the magazine clip into the .22. I caught up to her. She had just dug her keys out.

"Put your keys away Annabelle. The guns loaded." I flashed it to her. "You're going to give me your cell and we're going to take a walk."

The Confession of Annabelle

Annabelle put up a decent fight, but she was under the weather. She couldn't move like I could. I was skinny and swift, though a smoker. She was obese and slow. Her reflexes were not quick. She tried to whack me with her bag. That failed when her grip on it slipped and it went flying. I pulled the gun out of my waistband. I looked at her. "You're going to try that once more and I will put a bullet in between your eyes. Its question and answer time sweet Annabelle. No one's here. No one's going to hear you if you scream. Who was Alex to you? Answer honestly and I won't shoot you yet."

"He's my brother."

"Why did he take me Annabelle?"

"Because I set you up to be snatched."

"And why, Annabelle, why did you set me up?" She looked afraid. We were in the storage unit; there were a few hours before it was going to be busy on the streets enough to where people would see me. I needed things. I hit her and knocked her out. I left to go run a few errands at the few shops that were near here. I decided it was time to play with fire. I stopped at multiple amounts of stores. $40 here for paint thinner. $15 here for rags. This was to be my second fire in two days. I was ok with that. I went back and unlocked the door into the unit. She was awake. "Are you ready to talk now?" She nodded. "Tell me again how you know Alex." She admitted to Alex. He was her brother. How the hell they were related I did not know. It didn't matter anymore. He was dead. She needed to be as well. She confessed to me that she was a look out. She reported when there were new girls in town and ones that didn't have families or looked like they didn't have families to go home to.

"You were the perfect mark." She said that with how small I was she had figured he would have killed me early on. She was wrong. She didn't count on the fact that I had a brain and liked to read. While I was in jail I read about the human brain. What points to hit on the skull to knock a person out, what chemicals I needed to start a fire. I had kept my research quiet. I used logins that were stolen like from the stupid bitch from the prison lunch room. Her log in was easy to steal. They shouldn't let convicts on the computer. That was her fault, not mine. Maybe I should have left well enough alone; I didn't though. There was a score to settle. I had killed 12 people. I didn't care. I saved 7. It wasn't score for score anymore. It was survival and taking back what was mine. This bitch had taken my freedom for the last two years. I took her life as payment. He died. Now she was dead joining him in hell. There was a special place in hell reserved for her. I had my own special place reserved for me as well. However my story isn't done.

I created the same fire in the storage unit. I burned Annabelle's body like I burned her brother. I smiled. That made 12. I left the storage unit with everything inside that would have my hand prints on it. i walked out of the complex where they were all held.

Matthew

I started to wonder if I should tie up loose ends with her boyfriend as well. One more night here wouldn't hurt me. He would do one of two things. He would go looking for her, or cut his losses. He didn't seem like he was a strong person to be alone in life. So he would go looking for her and I needed to stop that. Since I had left no forwarding information with the hotel the only thing I needed was to break in there and take the file folder for myself. I needed plastic gloves. Maybe I would see if I could find a guest for the night where I could stay there. It would allow me to not arouse too much attention to myself. I didn't need them figuring out that little Rose was back; back and wanted for murder no less. Well they could pin my father's murder on me. The cop though. They might have a hard time with that one since he left with two hookers. They very well could have killed him. Money to a hooker was like crack to an addict. I would wait and find him before he went to the hotel if he was lucky. It might require me to stay awake for the day again. Forty-eight hours of no sleep wouldn't kill me. It wouldn't kill me to be nosey either. I should find someone who lived at the hotel as well. Maybe he, yes he you fool, would want to grab something to eat.

I could always put my job skills for the last two years to go use. They didn't need to know I had other motives. After I left the storage unit I found a place to eat. I went back to the coffee shop I passed on the way to the church. Why hadn't I applied here two years ago? It was quiet, small, and peaceful looking. There were a few people inside when I opened the door. A man with a mousey haired woman, they were eating quietly and not talking much.

There in the corner was an empty table. I walked over and set my back pack down, took out a $20, went to the counter, and ordered a coffee with 8 creamers and 8 sugars. The guy at the counter was cute. He looked like he was straight. He winked when I said 8 and 8.

"You need your coffee nice and sweet."

"Something like that" I told him." When he rang me up he asked if I wanted a bagel or muffin to add to my order. I hadn't had a real muffin in two years. I held my arm out. "You can twist it for a warm blueberry muffin with butter on the side." I was kind of surprised when he grabbed my arm and twisted it gently. He was a flirt. That could be good. I paid for everything and took my coffee and change to sit down while I waited for him to bring out the muffin. About seven minutes later he came around the corner of the counter and with a bit of gusto he placed the muffin on the table. He had put the butter in a small dish on the side, cut the muffin in half, and for garnish he had used some strawberries. "Wow does everyone get the royalty treatment? No ma'am you're new here. Next time you come in it won't be as special." I had to smile. He didn't have a name tag on. I had to wonder his name. He was polite. I didn't catch your name he asked. I looked up at him and smiled.

"It's Katie." This was going to be interesting. I'm sure I looked like shit and smelled god awful.

I would have to find a place to wash up. I needed a clean change of clothes too. "I don't see you have a name tag. You asked me for my name but I don't see yours."

"It's Matthew." He had on a band tee shirt, converse, and baggy jeans. He wasn't too big but he wasn't skinny. He filled the shirt out nicely. "It's weird Katie I've never seen you here before. A lot of the people who come here are regulars."

175

"I just got back to town. I haven't been here in two years. When I was here before it was only for a short amount of time."

"Well that sure makes sense. I moved here about a year and a half ago for school." He was a college boy. That explains his extra flirt. He then said he thought he knew all the pretty girls in town. Pretty girls in town. Yea he was a super flirt. Maybe it was for tips, or maybe it was for his kicks and getting laid.

He wouldn't be too happy if he knew I was a whore. Maybe he would who knew? He caught me staring into outer space while he kept talking. "So would you like to catch a movie Katie?" I came back down to earth.

"A movie?" I had to smile. That was cute of him to ask. Maybe he really was just a flirt. Maybe he didn't have real moves. "How old are you?" I had to ask him, ready for a small laugh to myself. He told me he was 21. That was a plus in his book. "This movie, what does it entail?"

"A date at the movie theater, popcorn, sodas, and candy, that sort of thing? Maybe after that I'll walk you home kiss you good night and go home."

"Kiss me? Aren't you hopeful? Yes I would love to join you for a movie, as for the rest we shall see how the night plays itself out." I handed him a napkin. "Write your number down for me. I don't have a phone. I'm planning on picking one up for myself later. Is there a local convenience store around here that sells them?" He looked up from writing his number down.

"There's one two blocks from here. When you're done with your muffin you should go check it out and see if they have something fitting for you."

"Then I guess we have a date. Though I think I should tell you I don't like horror movies, I prefer spy movies, or cop movies." He asked if a chick flick was out of the question. "Sure why not it's a date." There was a customer who came in.

"It's time for me to get back to work. I have 6 more hours in this place." I started to pick at my muffin and drink my coffee. These customers he knew and called them by name. He was a smart counter help. He made the customer feel welcome. I guess it's whatever got him tips. I guess he had needs as well. Maybe I would feel more like a human if I had mine met too in a subtle fashion. I picked at my muffin some and drank my coffee. He was a pro at making a cup though the blend was weak. I finished up what I could manage and left two dollars on the table as a tip for his service. I would see him later. Maybe I should use him to gain access to the hotel and book a room there. No I shouldn't do that. That might cause some red flags. On way my out the door I waved goodbye. He waggled his fingers at me like he was excited about our date later.

I picked up a paper on the way down the street. It was Sunday. Maybe they wouldn't notice the fire until more than one building was up in smoke. I had left all of the chemical bottles and rags in there so everything would burn faster including the prints that I had left on the bottles and cans. The guns were gone and with me. I really should leave here. Tonight. But I need to tie up loose ends. There's only so much I can hide without them catching on. At least for now. I'm an arsonist and a murderer. Just this information alone would have made the 16 year old me hide. I would have hidden in a hole and not wanted to come out. After seeing what the dirty world has done the switch in my head that had once made me care about every little thing was off. I saved those girls not two days ago. That was maybe a sliver of hope one my humanity being restored. After hearing Annabelle's confession I turned it off again. I would fake what I needed to for tonight for Matthew's sake. Then I would run. He needed to live. So hopefully the nice little college boy routine wasn't an act. He didn't need to be #14. My finger was itching to fire a gun again. Maybe he was a douche. Tonight would tell me. His fate would then be decided. I had some work cut out for me. I needed a shower new clothes and bleach for my entire body to be rid of the last two years of funk and regret and shame that I had no choice to bare. I would need to find clothing first. Nothing too pricey like I had gotten last time; just some leggings, new flats, and a shirt. That was my first stop. I needed to find a locker at the bus depot after that to stash my gun. First, time to stop at the gas station and get myself a new phone, and fast. That would make it easy to keep in contact with this boy. at least for tonight. My plans needed to go according to the plot in my head. Walking up the street there was a gas station on the right. I walked inside. There was a young girl at the counter. She looked like she was close to my age. She didn't say anything. She just watched me. There was an aisle with calling cards at the end were disposable cell phones with pre paid cards that you had to buy along with them so they would work.

I picked up a red box. It was cheap, $30 dollars for the phone, and $40 for the re-load card. I walked back up to the counter. This might take some texting to make this plan follow through for the night but I would learn how to make it happen over the course of the next few hours. I placed the items on the counter in front of her register. She looked at me with eyes like she didn't think I could afford this. I pulled my bag off of my shoulders and pulled a $100 out. "Can you please ring me up?" Her eyes betrayed her when she saw the hundred. She wasn't expecting it from a girl who looked like she was homeless. I've never mentioned this before but I have allergies. I couldn't smell myself. I'm sure I smelled glorious to her. She finished ringing me up and handed me the box and card.

"Would you like a bag?"

"No thanks I have my own." She counted my change back to me, I thought for a few moments while I was here I should grab soap and a small thing of deodorant and a brush. I needed a brush. I should smell clean. Flowery and clean. No, just clean. Why he asked me for a date when I looked homeless I had no idea, but whatever.

He was weird and he would use me for a date so I would use him for a cover as to where I was.

After it was done I would head to the bus depot and call Viv to see if I could meet her somewhere. Maybe I would blow $100 to take a cab so I could meet her closer so she didn't have to drive. I'm sure she would appreciate that. I wouldn't have to smell her weed for 30 minutes. I would get a hotel room so I could have some peace and quiet. I had to wonder what her life was like, if she had a family someone to take care of, or if she was a washed up stoner. You know I shouldn't judge. I've been with close to a hundred men. I could be ridden with STDs. Some of them didn't strap on a rubber when they fucked me. Skin on skin. One of them said his wife couldn't and wouldn't have kids with him so he made sure he didn't wear a condom with me. He wanted a child so badly that he paid out the asshole for a hooker to try and get them knocked up. The only good thing about Alex was that he supplied the morning after pill. I had heard that he had taken a girl out back and killed her and burned her body when a date had gotten her knocked up. The baby wouldn't have stood a chance, since she was a heroin addict. Her date shot up with her on a regular basis. I digress. I left the store after I made that last purchase.

I went down the road about 3 blocks. There was a clothing shop with an open sign on the door. I walked in. the clerk who was at the desk looked at me like I wanted to rob the place. I just smiled. "Can I leave my bag with you? I've had a rough couple of days. I need some new clothes. I need to find a shower so I can feel like a human again." She nodded. I shrugged my bag off and handed it to her. The safety was on the gun while it was in my backpack. There wasn't a chance of it going off if she wasn't careful and just dropped the bag.

"What kind of clothes are you looking for miss? Some leggings? Maybe some baggy shirts. Some flats oh and undies. The whole 9 yards." She looked at me like I was crazy. I looked back at her.

"Sweetie I was held against my will for the last two years of my life. I need new clothes and then I'm going to find a room for rent, shower the longest hottest shower of my life, and sleep for a few hours in a clean bed." She looked at me. "Why don't you hand me my bag sweetie. If you think money is going to be an issue. I'll show you I can clearly afford what I need." Almost as if to challenge me I thought she backed up to the counter. She picked up my bag and handed it to me. I set it on the counter. Unzipped it slowly. The money wad wasn't hard to find, it was close to the top. I grabbed it and took it out. "I'll be paying in cash," as I flashed the wad of money to her eyes. There were two hundreds that protruded out. Her eyes were looking right at them.

"I guess I was wrong to judge you. I am sorry. We have everything you need right here. What size shoe did you say you needed?"

"I didn't."

She was a snot. I wondered if she worked on minimum wage. I put the wad of cash in my shorts pocket. She did look at it a little too much. The clerk snapped into place as a busy body. "Did you have a color legging that you liked?"

"Black would be great."

"Do you like any colors?" I looked at her.

"What do you mean?"

"I mean for your shirts?" I'm sorry she apologized "I should have said that to begin with. Do you have any plain black flats?"

"I like blue red and black. Maybe you have rock tee shirts or anything with skulls." She looked at me sideways "I have a few ideas for you. It looks like you're an extra small for the leggings."

"No I need a small," I told her. "A small in the underwear and maybe a large in tee shirts. I prefer room." She picked up 3 pairs of leggings.

"Here, all black like you requested. Here are two red shirts one with a heart and dagger driven through it. The other is plain. There are two black shirts for you to choose from as well. One plain and the other with a skull print on it.

"I'd like all four." She set them on the counter. I went to the underwear table picked up two thongs and two pairs of cotton boy briefs. She took them from me and set them on the counter. There was a short denim skirt. "I'd really like that skirt in a small." It was on the mannequin in the window.

"I think that's the last one," she said. "Let me check it. She got the mannequin down to check the tag. She took the skirt off. "You're in luck, it is a small." She handed it to me. You have three outfits and a skirt. Here are the shoes we have. She showed me three black pairs. Two had buckles and other one was plain.

"I'd like the plain in a size 8." She went to the counter went behind it. She came back with a box and showed me they were both an 8. "A basic black purse, and a new backpack, do you have those?"

"Yes I am sure we do. Let me get them for you from the backroom." She came back with two things in her hands. That was everything I needed.

I smiled, "That's everything." She smiled back.

"Ok let's go get you rung up." Her take on cheerfulness made me want to puke. I had to deal with it. Just for a few more minutes. The clothes were cheap and needed. They would fit me and I would make it work.

"I have one more question. Is there a cheap hotel or motel around here?"

"About 3 blocks down the way." That was near my old hotel. I had forgotten there was a no-tell motel.

"Do they rent rooms?" She looked at me. She had secrets you could tell. She played it off like she wasn't sure. She told me she thought so. I told her thanks and I would go check it out. My bill came to a total of $125.00 for everything. She placed everything in a shopping bag. She apologized again for being so rude when I first walked in. I smiled as sweetly as I could. "Well we all make mistakes, don't we?" She nodded. I would guess that she was grateful I didn't make a bigger stink than I already had. Karma had a way of screwing people the way they had already screwed others. She would get what was coming to her in the end. We all would. I left the shop.

I went three blocks down. Thankfully, the no-tell motel was before the other hotel. This was a good thing. I walked in through the doors and up to the counter. He gave me a look, like he thought I was trouble. That was fine. He could think that. I needed a room for the day and the night too. "I noticed you charge by the hour. What's the rate for one whole day? 24 hours from now."

"Check out tomorrow morning. $150 cash rate. No questions asked, and the rooms are clean?" He looked at me with eyes like who was I to ask if the room was clean. I removed the sweetness from my eyes. "Look, I've been through hell. I just want to know the room I'm going to has clean sheets on the bed. I really don't want to go in there and lay down on a dirty cum stained bed."

He just looked at me. "Yes there's a maid who goes in and cleans the beds. Even if the rooms only been used for an hour. There is indeed a maid. The sheets are clean the shower is bleached. Do you want the room or not?" I still had the money in my pocket from the clothes shop.

"Here's $150 there's an extra $50 in it for you if you forget I was here, and maybe $50 more if you erase your security camera."

He looked at me. "Make it $200 extra and ill have the maid bring you fresh soap and towels in the morning." I had to laugh.

"You're serious? Fresh soap and towels in the morning throw in coffee as well and you have a deal. And not the shit coffee from a drip. Nothing weak. From the coffee house six blocks west of here. And you will get your $200 when I leave here. That way I can make sure that you follow up on your end of the deal. We can shake on this deal if you like." He extended his boney arm and put it out to where I was able to comply with a handshake. I shook his hand firmly. Regardless if I was just as skinny as he was from the last two years of abuse that my body endured, I would break him if he fucked me over. I smiled at him sweetly. "There's $150," as I counted out the cash for him. I set the money on the counter. He got the keys ready for the room.

"Ok you're all set your check out time is noon tomorrow. I'll make sure I knock at 10 am with your coffee. That's what time my shift starts." He set the keys on the counter. "You don't have a lot of bags. So it doesn't look like you're going to need a lot of help getting upstairs."

"No." I picked the keys up. Room 216. That was a nice number. "Thanks," I looked at his name tag, "Thanks Luke." What was it with everyone having biblical names today? Did their parents think it would help them from paving their own personal roads to hell?

"Out the door, up the stairs, and to the left. If you go right you will run into a dead end. I only say this because there are some women, well, they don't pay attention." He smiled as nicely as he could manage.

I took the keys went outside with my knapsack and bag and went upstairs and to the room. Unlocked it quickly and went inside.

Maybe I was too hard on him. You could actually smell the bleach in there. There wasn't any dust either. Maybe they did things differently down south. I set my clothes bag on the desk and the ratty backpack as well. Time to unzip the backpack I need to get the cell phone programmed. I sat down on the floor to get the box open. I opened the instructions and plugged the phone in. There was a small scratch bar on the back of the card. I dug in my pocket for a coin to rub the silver off. There was a long 16 digit code uncovered. When I turned the phone on I programmed the number in there. I powered it off and back on. I opened the booklet to read where to find the number in there. I took it wrote it down on a separate piece of paper. I found Matthew's number in my pocket. I had never sent a text before. Texting was something that came out when I was stuck in the warehouse. When I dialed the number an envelope picture popped up if I wanted to send a text. I pressed the button and typed that it was Katie. We had met in the coffee shop this was my number he could contact me here. He must have been on break. He messaged me right back. Mind you, I haven't really used computers in a while. It took me a moment to figure out that he had put a smiley face on one of the messages. He told me he was off at 6. He would call me after he went home and got cleaned up. I needed a shower.

That was the first order of business. I went into the bathroom. I was surprised to see how clean it was. I turned the water on to let it warm up and went out to get my things. I got out the shampoo and conditioner and hair brush. There were little soap bars in there already. I intended on using both of them. The shower heated up pretty fast when I went back in there it was nice and steamy. I would enjoy this. I got in and sat under the shower stream for 30 minutes to let every single pore in my body open up. After that, I grabbed the soap and scrubbed myself as hard as I could. By the time I was done my skin was bright pink. I got out dried my hair and got dressed. The new clothes felt amazing. I cut the tags on everything. I opened up the new bag I got from the clothes shop. I cleaned out the money from the bag and my ID. I would burn the fuck out of the old bag tonight when I caught up with Annabelle's boyfriend. I should have burned it to a crisp when I burned Annabelle. I would soak it in gasoline when I killed her slime bag boyfriend. There was a video camera in the hotel lobby. I would find where the office was so I could destroy the system. I began to towel dry my hair off again and started to brush through it. Maybe the final piece of the puzzle was to get my hair cut. A little primping never hurt anyone. I smirked; Matthew was a nice boy. If I had feelings I would regret it. But he was a man whore. I was sure of it. I braided my hair down my back. He was worth a new outfit and a clean body that was it.

The phone blinked about an hour later. It was Matthew, he smiley faced me again. He was to be off work in an hour. He wanted to meet up at the movie theater. I texted him back that I was hungry for more than popcorn. We bantered back and forth for about 3 messages and said that there was a pizza place 3 blocks from here. He would need an hour to go to his place and clean up. He would meet me there. It was almost too good to be true. Annabelle was dead. Her scumbag would die. The video recorder; I would have to find the main server. I would break it and set it afire. There were a few more things that I needed. I didn't have any makeup. Maybe I should see if there's a lip-gloss or chapstick at the convenience store on the corner. I grabbed the key and the bag with the money and quickly ran out.

The store clerk looked at me. "You cleaned up."

"You're right I did." She was a bit nicer. I grabbed an extra stick of deodorant and soap while I was in there. I would need them. I checked the time. I had 30 minutes. The lip-gloss was cheap, the soap wasn't. I paid quickly and left. I needed to drop my things off in the storage locker and take the money and purse with me. No matter what, I wasn't leaving that there. If the dirt bag clerk decided that he wanted to check the room he didn't need to find all the money I had. I was ready. Matthew, ready or not, tonight will be one night you won't forget. I put the DND sign out locked the door. I wouldn't be late.

Burning Down the House

When I got down to the hotel lobby the manager was there. "You're back again."

"I am indeed." Matthew was sleeping upstairs none the wiser.

"How did you get in?"

"A friend let me in. We spent a lovely evening out and fell asleep watching a movie. I came down here. I wanted to ask Annabelle a few more questions. She gave me a funny look. You know like she knew something more than she was saying about my abduction. She isn't here and she isn't answering her cell either. It keeps going directly to voicemail. Maybe she forgot to charge it when she got home from work." I looked at him with big blue eyes and smiled.

"What kind of questions?"

"When I asked her if she knew Alex, my abductor, she had a look of fear in her eyes. Almost like she knew something." He told me she had a brother. She never really talked about him. I looked at him. "Why don't you lock the door and we go in your office and we talk about everything. I think you know more than you're saying." He went to move. I pulled the gun from my purse. "I don't think so. Now get your keys lock the fucking door and move quickly." He actually looked scared. That wasn't a bad thing. The clip was fully loaded. It wasn't my gun. It was Alex's. The one I had stolen from the safe. It wasn't something they could trace back to me. He went towards the counter and I pulled the gun back to load the chamber. "Are you really willing to test me? I will blow your goddamn brains out right here and now." I wasn't loud when I said it. I was very quiet and point blank. His eyes got really wide. I think that must have hit home that I was serious. I would kill him tonight. I watched his movement when he came around the counter. He had his keys in his hand and locked the door. "I'll follow you to the office." I gave him a look like if you move near the alarm system will blow your brains out. He stopped. I said, "Move." I didn't yell I didn't know if there were guests on the first floor. "Go through the office. Go to the file cabinet. Get my folder. I want all of it. The whole thing is coming with me tonight."

"You're a crazy bitch you know that?"

"Yes I know. And your problem is you helped create part of it. You and your girl. You set me up to get taken from the street. You both profited from it with money."

He looked back. "Money? It was from girls?"

"You didn't know? It certainly wasn't from an inheritance she received; now get the fucking file folder and move before I blow your brains out right here." He grabbed the file folder and went to the door that leads to his office. We went up the stairs and to the right. There was a TV and two players. "Open them," I said. He did I removed the discs that were inside of each of them. "Where is the backup hard drive located? He opened up a desk drawer. There was a modem inside. That will do. What else is it attached to? Does it run anything other than the security system? No that's the only thing it holds. Unplug it. Find a bag and give it to me. A bag? Are you out of your mind? You're kidding me. No you idiot, that's not something I do. The hard drive and all the data are coming with me. And you look like a perverse type. So I would make sure that any back up disks that you have are all given over as well. I want all the pictures and the scan prints of women who have been in and out of this hotel. The ones you jerk off to while your bitch is down stairs."

He looked at me like a light went off in his head. "H-h-how did you know that."

"Because you look like the type of scumbag that would do that. You didn't have to validate it for me. You need to understand this you pig. Tonight you're going to die. You're a pervert and you helped aide human sex trafficking. There's no way you didn't know about it. You questioned Annabelle where the money came from. I know you did. You're a nosey prick. I'm sure you made suggestions as to who looked like an easy mark." He was scared. There was no denying I was right. He had helped. He thought I was an over privileged brat who ran away from her hometown. He was a skinny little fuck but he was scared. I focused more back on him. "Get this shit ready to go. Now! Don't touch any keys just pull the plugs and bag it up now." He went to the back of the tower. He started to slowly unplug everything. Hurry up asshole. I pressed the barrel of the gun to the back of his head. He started to unplug things faster. He had a back pack attached to the back of the door. He got it down when he was he was done unplugging everything. He stuffed the hard drive in there and zipped it up.

"Here you go bitch." I kicked him hard right in the groin when he handed it to me. He fumbled.

"You need to watch your manners asshole."

"You're going to kill me so what's the point."

"You stupid fuck of course I'm going to kill you but if you showed some remorse I would make it easier on you. Instead I'm going to make you suffer. You have nothing more to lose. You have no idea what you helped put me through. Would you want to be kidnapped drugged and raped? They would make you a real pretty girl in a sex slave trade. I'm sure there'd be someone who would turn you out. Put his dick in your ass. Unless you've done it already. Maybe that's your kink, I really don't care. You won't have more kinks. Now, close the door asshole and turn the volume up on the TV in here. I don't want anyone to hear the gun going off. Or maybe we should take a walk down the hall to a cleaning closet and find something flammable to play with. How would you like to die tonight? A bullet to the back of the head? Do you want to ingest some paint thinner? Some bleach? He looked at me again.

"You really are a sick bitch." I laughed.

"You have no idea how sick I am. Walk!" I jammed the barrel of the gun into the back of his neck. "Walk asshole. No tricks. Walk now." He went forward more out the door and down the hall avoiding the stairs we had come up moments before. There's a utility closet not far down from here."

"How did you know that?"

"Because you idiot I lived here for a few weeks don't you think I walked the halls when I couldn't sleep? This hotel has cracks and crevices. To a young mind you have to find where things are. Where you can go. What doors open and what don't. You didn't have a decent cleaning crew on duty at the time. They left a lot of things unlocked at times. You have a few closets throughout the hotel. One could make a real mess of things if you aren't careful. There's a switch box on the third floor we can go there and cut the wires. After that we can pour some cleaning chemicals on there and light a match. The fire alarms would start going off and no one would hear the gun fire. Now walk asshole. Time's wasting. It's time for you to die. And if you make a single peep to alert people it will be that much more painful. You're going to watch more people than just yourself die tonight. Open the door to the closet, now. Start getting the chemicals out. We're going to the switch box. You're a lucky boy. I have a lighter on me as well. I jammed the gun in his back again. Get the paint thinner and the bleach bottle out.

We're going to take that and go upstairs. Get the rags as well. We're going to take the stairs up to the third floor and go to the switch box."

"You're a crazy bitch... the cops are gonna find you. You'll go to prison."

"They might. But by then you'll be in hell where you belong with all the rest of them. So prison. You see I've been to prison. I was a hero. I shot my dad for beating my mother with the intent to kill him for hurting her." He faced me. "Yes I can hear the wheels in your head turning. You see before you and your fat ass had me taken off the street I was a criminal just wanting to hide. You fucked that up. It would have been a nice quiet little life too, as much as you don't want to hear this. But maybe you should understand what I took away from other people in order to get here the first time. But that would take more than half the brain that you have in your skull and none of what you have in your pants in order to understand." The stairs were unoccupied and it was late at night or early in the morning however you want to look at it. "Walk asshole, up the stairs to the third floor. Don't try anything silly while you're going up either, I will shoot you and then light this bitch up faster than you know what to do with your flaccid penis. You have two flights of stairs to go up so walk quickly. He quickened his pace."

"You could spare me. I won't tell anyone."

"I highly doubt that. You're a pussy of a man with no backbone. You would fold quicker than a deck of cards and sing like a stuck pig that's headed to the butcher block the minute a cop looked at you sideways." He made it up one flight quickly and stopped for a second to catch his breath like he was asthmatic. "Move asshole!" I yelled at him. He started crying. He started moving again. The switchbox was just around the corner from the stairwell door. One flight of stairs left. The fire alarms needed to go off before I shot him in the head. He had a pad of paper in his pocket I noticed while

I was behind him. I made him stop one more time he needed to write a note saying good bye as to why he killed himself. If the fire didn't burn the note alive they would see where he crumbled and couldn't live with himself. He couldn't live with the pain he suffered knowing he helped take innocent girls off the street. "Now put it back in your pocket asshole. When they strip you down they will find it. Up, up the stairs you go. You have to say good night moon for the last time." He was up the stairs quickly as he wrote the note against his will. He started to realize that this was the end. "Open the door shit head." He opened it and it swung open enough for me to walk out directly behind him. The door swung closed and the switch box was less than 5 steps away." Open it, and cut wires that won't alert anyone who might be awake right now. Cut the wires for the basement no one is awake down there accept the rats which is where I should have taken you to begin with. Open the paint thinner and put the rags in there." He did just as he was told trembling and splashing it all over himself. "Toss the rags out where they should be just far enough to where they will catch on fire quickly." I made him toss the rags down away from the stair well. I still needed to get the hell out of here before the night was over and I burned alive with him. Put the paint thinner down you have some dripped on you as well dummy. I took my lighter out of my pocket and flicked it on. I bent down to the rag to light it up. "There's one." I went to the cut wires. "There's two and the fire alarm went off." Ahhh music to my ears. I pulled the gun close to his head. Right in the middle of his eyes. "We're done here." He closed his eyes and I pulled the trigger. I watched him fall down to the floor like a limp rag. It was time to depart. I ran downstairs with the bag and the tower. There was a fire door on the bottom floor. Just a few more steps and I was there. I could hear people yelling upstairs that they needed to call the fire department. One more step and I'd be at the door. My hand slammed against it and it opened. I was out.

Freedom Was a Cab Ride Away

I left the hotel and hailed a cab. There was one parked close to the hotel. "Where are we headed miss?" I shoved the tower into the back of the cab and got inside. The cabbie was male. He looked into the back seat at me. "Where to?" He asked again.

"The bus depot and then we're taking a ride out of town."

"You have enough money for that kind of trip?" He just looked at me.

"I don't think you need to worry about money. I have enough to cover the trip and to tip you as well. Before we go to the bus depot I need you to turn this cab around to go back to the no tell motel that was next to the hotel. I need to grab my bag. After that our long drive can begin."

"What assurances do I have that you aren't going to leave and run?"

"I can leave the tower in here and give you a fresh hundred if that would make you feel better." He nodded in agreement. I took the hundred out of my purse and got out of the cab when he parked in front of the motel. I handed it to him. "Wait here. I'll be back." I ran upstairs and grabbed everything from the room. I was taking the new clothes. They were mine. I earned them. The money

I had stolen from the safe was still in my purse. I grabbed my new bag. There was no time to do a clean sweep of the room. I ran to the desk and grabbed a piece of paper. Time to leave the geek sleaze a note. It read something like; sorry I couldn't stay for coffee. I dropped an extra $300 on the table and grabbed anything that had a trace of me on there. He would be less than understanding but if I hoped enough he would keep his end of the deal with the extra money on the table. That would have to make do. I scribbled one more line that there was $300 on the table so if the cleaning lady got there first she would be less inclined to take it. I left the key on the table and walked out the door. The cabbie better still be down stairs I thought. I flew down the stairs. Thankfully, the cab was still there. I threw my bag in the back and hopped in." To the bus depot. Now." He took the car out of park and went three blocks down the way. "Stop here and wait." I got out again made sure my purse was with me. I ran into the bus depot and got everything that was in the locker out of there. I took the other gun and tucked it into my waist band and turned around to leave there were two guns with me now. I made it quickly out of there and back to the cab. This asshole better not try to touch me on the way there. I would spare no effort when I put as many bullets as both chambers would allow into his skull. I would take my money back that I fronted him as well. I got into the cab. I had been out of the hotel for 15 minutes which was enough time before someone noticed the small fire I had started in his office and call 911. That would mean that there would be sirens any moment. "Drive. We're headed 30 minutes north of here." I figured maybe 5 more minutes before road blocks went up. Those road blocks would keep us from leaving and going anywhere.

"Yes ma'am." He put the taxi in drive and put his foot on the gas.

"Just don't do anything stupid to get us stopped mister. I need away from this hell hole of a city." He didn't say a word for awhile he just drove. When we were about 10 minutes away. You could hear sirens in the night air from the distance. He turned his head slightly to the side.

"Those sirens… are they for you?"

"No mister."

"I don't need any drama on my taxi license."

"You won't mister. Just get on the freeway and I'll tell you where you need to go from there and where we need to get off." When we got close I sent Viv a text to let her know I had wrapped up my business in St Louis. I shifted in my seat carefully to take the gun out of my waistband without making the driver aware of what I was doing. If he did notice what I was doing there wouldn't be time for him to pull over and stop. I would have to put a bullet in his head and pray I could try and stop the cab before it crashed. I wouldn't be able to explain a cab on fire either. That would be the only way that I would be able to rid the proof I was in that car though. We would just have to see how the next half an hour played itself out.

My phone blinked. It was Viv. She wasn't there. That wasn't a problem. I texted back that I would go and find a diner close and wait there. I sent another text. What exit did I need to use? She texted me back right away, with the correct exit. It sounded like I would be wide awake for a while. No nap tonight. There was too much blood rushing through my veins. Maybe she would smoke me out again. It would help me come down from the adrenaline high.

"Miss," he interrupted my thoughts. "Do you know how much this cab ride is going to cost you?" I looked at the meter it was sitting at $22.78 and growing rapidly.

"What I fronted you about 20 minutes ago will cover most of it. Don't worry mister I will be able to pay my fare." I settled back in after the second gun was stowed in my bag. I had made sure the safety was on. I looked out the window and watched the lights along with the long haul trucks on the freeway.

He asked if I wanted some music. "Sure what do you like?"

"I'm 57 years old miss. I'm out here supporting my daughter and little grandson who just moved home with my wife and me. I like Coltrane. It relaxes me for some reason."

"Coltrane it is then. I don't need a jumpy cabbie." He put the radio on and plugged in a CD player without taking his eyes off the road. He turned the speakers up to a medium level and hit play all the while not taking his eyes off the road ahead. He had done this before.

Grandson and daughter. He needed to go home to them. Tip him extra Rosie. That way he can afford to take tomorrow night off. That is indeed what I would do without a doubt. The driver asked if I needed any air. I told him I was fine. He asked if I minded a little wind coming from his window while he smoked. I asked if I could have one too. The driver chuckled. As long as you don't tell my boss we did, I don't see an issue. I took my cigarettes out of the bag and lit one up as I rolled down the window.

"You don't seem like you're from around here miss."

"I'm not, I'm from all over. I'm going to stay with some family right now. I had a bad break up with my boyfriend. I was able to get out with the tower when I went to try and pick up the rest of my things. That's why I only have a backpack. He destroyed the rest of my things."

That was what pulled on his heart strings. "You're a brave girl," he told me. "There's about a 15 minute more ride for you. We will be at your stop."

"Thank you mister."

"It's Lenny miss. My name is Lenny."

"Mine is Laura." I was paying in cash so he wouldn't ask for ID. I've learned to lie pretty well by now. Even if he was a smart old man. He didn't question anything.

He had calmed down a lot it seemed once we were out of the city. The Coltrane helped him calm down a little more. That would work out well for me. No questions and $300 in his pocket. Maybe it would take him home for a week so he could spend time with his family. I didn't know. But I did know that for once today I was doing the right thing. One right thing wouldn't make up for the countless wrong things I've done in my life. But maybe just maybe it would soften the blow when it came time for judgment day. Probably not. But I could dream.

I checked my phone for messages. This whole phone thing was new to me. I didn't have one before I went to jail. I didn't know half of the shit I was doing. There was a new message from Viv. She said that there was a 24 hour restaurant three blocks from her house called Tino's. I was to wait for her there. She also said to smile really big at the waiter and he would give me endless cups of coffee. I needed to get out on exit 54 and then go three blocks north and one block east. The restaurant would be there. I looked out the window. We were at exit 51. "Lenny could you exit at 54 and go three blocks north please?"

"Sure, you've been a real pleasure to have in my cab. No worries. "I guess I couldn't complain about that. Someone showed me kindness. I would continue to show them kindness in turn. He turned where he was supposed to off the freeway and then I told him to go three blocks north like she told me and one block east. He pulled up within 10 minutes. I got out and went to his window to pay after I pulled the tower out from the seat behind him. I handed him the $300. He told me that was too much. I looked at him kindly.

"Maybe that will pay your cab rent for the week so you can keep your tips. Maybe even afford a night off with your daughter and your grand baby. They need you too. You're a gentleman. Have a safe ride back into the city."

"God bless you miss." He looked at me one more time before he put the car in reverse and left me out there. I was here. It was time for the endless coffee until chatterbox got there.

Raid

They raided the den. There were 15 cops. Viv was tackled and she resisted arrest. All I heard was her scream. "Katherine run!" I was so fucking high it wasn't funny. I just sat down and didn't move.

The cops there surrounded me. "Put your hands behind your head. Move slowly. No sudden moves." I laid down on my stomach. I put my hands up behind my head. The cop came up behind me. And put my arms down by my waist he pulled out a pair of zip ties out. He took my wrists and cuffed me with them. "You're going to get up slowly. You have the right to remain silent. Anything you say can and will be held against you in a court of law. You have the right to an attorney. If you cannot afford an attorney one will be appointed for you. Do you understand these rights as I have read them to you?"

I giggled "Yes." Then I giggled "Do you know that you're the only cop that's ever read them to me before? And I've been arrested before. I was in prison. But I was never mirandized." I was so high I just laughed.

The cop pulled me up. "Let's go." I didn't fight him. He didn't jerk me around. I was high as a kite. We had smoked about two of Viv's joints. We had also done lines and laughed hard all day. I didn't have a care in the world. I would later when I came down. I heard the cop say to his partner that my prints needed to be run. I had admitted that I was a criminal. I heard his partner say that this was a nice bust they had 3 convicted perps; one fresh meat. Fresh perp she meant me. Well we'll see if she's fresh. This day just gets better and better. She laughed, he snorted. "We did good work today. There's about $10,000 dollars here in cash. 2 ounces of coke and there were about 3 ounces of weed too." The list went on with assorted pill bottles. The only guy who was arrested was the same guy I gave a blow job too earlier. You could call him my dealer. We had an arrangement; drugs for sex. He was stingy he got a lot more blow jobs than I got joints but it was whatever. Up until today I was hidden from the world with no cares either. I should care right now but I didn't. I was getting into the back of a squad car. His partner had Viv. They got her when she was on her way out the back door. I had a seat next to her.

She asked me, "How could you not run?"

"Run?" I giggled. "I can't even think straight enough to walk." Thinking about that made me laugh more.

The cops got into the front of the squad car. "Ladies you are headed to jail. I would suggest being very quiet unless you want something special going into our reports." Viv told the officer to fuck off.

The officer pissed her off with what he said next. "No thanks I'm afraid even with a shower, penicillin and a few other choice drugs you wouldn't interest me with a hundred foot pole put between the two of us." She screamed that he has a dirty piece of shit. The female partner looked back through the cage.

"You need to calm down now." The female cop looked like she wasn't kidding. She was small but looked tough. She got on the radio and called her dispatch. "This is car 2529 we're in route with two female perps. One is going to need a strait jacket she's high as a kite on god knows what. I don't want anyone to be a vic when she comes down. Her prints need to be run as well. She's new to our system but it sounds like she has priors."

199

"You little lying cunt you have priors?!" Viv screamed. "You were a sex slave."

I just laughed. "Yes I was. But you never asked what came before that. Not once. So shut the fuck up you idiotic bitch before you get into more trouble like mine," I began to laugh again. I didn't care, she was a dumb coke whore and I was tired of listening to her whine. We were close to the police station.

"You girls are close to your new home. We're going to get you processed and in cells for the rest of the night. The little one is going in a cell by herself so if she turns violent when she comes down from whatever the hell she ingested today." The female cop said that twice, once on the radio to her dispatch. And now for her partner to hear. I suppose it was for us also.

"Before we left did you see if there were any candy bars in the vending machine?" he asked her.

The female cop spoke up, "You idiot. Just go in my desk drawer there's juice boxes and chocolate as well as fruit snacks in there. Remember I'm diabetic."

"I forget, I'm sorry." As soon as we get there she will be processed. When she comes down we can interrogate her and feed her. A little bit of what's in your stash to keep her sugar level up so she doesn't crash.

He said, "For some reason I don't think we're going to have to worry about her crashing. I think we're going to have to worry about what we find on her record when we run her prints." We got closer to the police station and the cops said that there were people who would meet us. They were more worried about being able to control Viv than they were me. It seemed a little ridiculous but what happened would happen. If they knew what I was or who I was they would ship me back to Chicago. Sweet home Chicago. No, I didn't want to go back there. We reached the station. There were eight people out there waiting. Funny, the eight people were for her. The cop and his female partner dragged me in by themselves. They went through the gate and stopped at the finger print area in booking. There were computers. No finger print ink was required. I looked at them.

"I have to go to the bathroom." The female cop said I could hold it until they were done with my prints. I was done. My two and a half years of freedom were over. I started laughing again. It didn't matter, as all good things must come to an end. She was done running my prints.

"Let's go." She took me to the bathroom. "You're gonna have to figure this one out sweetie." Considering all I had on were some panties and a long tee-shirt. Maybe it wouldn't be hard. But there was a stall. I couldn't close the door. Are you serious? I was not a happy girl. The female cop looked at me. "You better hurry up and pee princess. It's gonna be a long night in lock up. I sure as hell don't want to be around when you come down."

"Officer, ma'am..." I squinted to see if she had a name badge on. "I admit I'm guilty of a lot of things. But right now. I'm high as a kite. I'm about to piss myself so if you could unwedge your thong from your ass and help I'd be thankful."

#

I had been there in jail for two days. During the middle of the night a guard came to the door while I was hovered over the toilet. He yelled at me to get up. I was being moved.

"You're headed to prison. We ran your prints. You have a rap sheet little one." He opened the cell door and came in. "Get up". He slapped the cuffs on me and jerked me up from the floor. "Let's go princess. They'll give you a bag in the paddy wagon that you can puke in." I bent over and wretched again.

"Just fucking kill me."

"Oh little girl where you're going you will wish that death could come fast." With that being said he yanked me up again. "Let's go princess." He walked, jerking me out of the cell. "Prisoner 842367 is being moved", he spoke into his radio. "There's an escort to the bus needed. Meet me at the next gate. Make sure there's a barf bag with you as well for the little princess. She's coming down from whatever she ingested at the den you busted her at. Whatever is coming out of her is techni-color. She's a bit pasty too. You might consider bringing her some OJ as well for when she stops puking out everything that's in her stomach. Make sure there are guards posted throughout the jail. There needs to be two guards on the bus as well. She might sit there in a veggie state but we don't need to take any chances." 10-4 was all that came over the radio.

"Where the hell are you taking me?"

"You'll find out soon enough princess. You are a killer. In your drugged state you admitted to many crimes. That includes murder and prostitution." We had made it down the hall with him half dragging me like a rag doll. There were two guards at the next gate. "Open up I need to take her to the bus; she's being transported back to Chicago." They opened the gate and didn't ask questions. "We're almost to processing. Thankfully for you, I got all of your transport paperwork ready before I came and got you. That will speed up the transport. It's going to be a long bus ride." We went upstairs. Processing was on the right. There was the door and you could see the bus outside. He looked at the desk officer. "She's being taken out to the bus and transported back to Chicago tonight." The desk sergeant nodded. Didn't ask any questions and went back to the scrabble game that she was working on.

We went outside and boarded the bus. The first seat had a guard in it so I went to the third one back and stumbled into the seat. I got situated. The driver got up and closed the gate between the bus entry and the passenger area. The driver sat back down and started the bus. "We have a long drive everyone buckle up and get comfy." He pulled the bus out of the lot. We were about 3 blocks away when the guard who was in the back got up and moved closer to the front. I didn't look around to see what they were doing. About 10 minutes passed by the guard got up again and came over to me to make sure that my cuffs were secure. After he checked them he pulled out a hood and pulled it over my head. After that I felt a needle go in my arm. That was when everything went black.

About the Author

Shannon Anton is currently enrolled in Northwestern College studying for a degree in the medical field. She is married and the mother of one. Shannon resides in Chicago, Illinois.

Shannon is a DJ and a writer. She has deep obsession with many different styles of writing implements and coffee.

The Madness of Rose
Dark Diaries Trilogy

By Shannon Anton
Stellium Books

Book 1

My Name is Rose: Diary of a Serial Killer

Fall 2015

Book 2

Waking Up the Devil

2016

Book 3

Even the Devil has to Pay Her Dues

2016

More Thrillers and Paranormal Reads
New From Stellium Books 2015
www.stelliumbooks.com

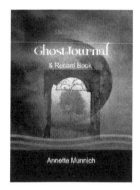

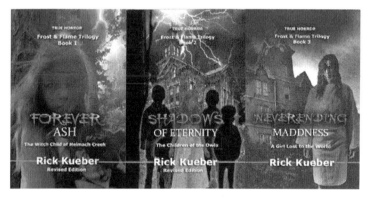

Made in the USA
Charleston, SC
11 November 2016